Deprogramming
A Bully

Deprogramming

A Bully

THE BARBER CHAIR SERIES ~ BOOK 1

—∿∿—

Kathy Rae

The Barber Chair Series ~ Book 1: Deprogramming A Bully
Copyright © 2017 by Kathy Rae. All rights reserved.

This is a publication of K.Rae Kreations.

Published in the United States of America
ISBN-13: 978-0-996583008
ISBN-10: 0-996583009

1. Juvenile Fiction / Action & Adventure / General
2. Juvenile Fiction / Social Themes / Bullying

To the thousands of people
who have blessed me
by sitting in my barber chair.

And
*To You, **my Jesus**,*
I give You all the glory!

Acknowledgements

Thank you to the following people for the help you gave to produce this book:

Mike Curnutt for information concerning juvenile correction in Bingham County of Idaho State.

Jon Christensen, Robin Smick, Peggy Stears and Sheryl High
for your constant encouragement.

Aprilily (http://aprilily21.webs.com)
for designing a great book cover.

Julia Ockerman for a great job of proofreading.

Cheryl Foster for the tour of Shelley High School.

Matthew Broadhead for being an honest friend while preparing the book for narration.

My dad and mom, **Vern and Dorothy Elder,** for guidance in decisions concerning publication of this book and for every form of support possible to make my dream come true.
I love you!

Content

Table of Contents

Prologue

"Logan?" A voice whispered in the darkness. "Lo-gan..."

Logan's head slumped to his chest then snapped upright with eyes wide open. He didn't remember falling asleep. The uneasiness of the dream lingered as Logan tried to remember what it was about. His wet palms skidded across the brown leather on his barber chair. His pulse was slowing with the comfort of his surroundings.

Then a commanding voice spoke. "Logan."

He turned to the waiting room and hurdled out of the chair onto his knees.

Light overwhelmed every inch of the barbershop. The Angel was cloaked in the purest white, almost diamond-like. His head touched the nine-foot ceiling. A gentle smile appeared, accentuating the love permeating his eyes. "Rise, Logan. I am a mere messenger of the Lord."

"Why are you here?" Logan stood.

"The Lord God knows of your servant's heart. He is sending children to you who need help with difficulties they face."

"Tell me what I need to do, and I'll do it."

"When a child comes for a haircut and asks, 'How high does this chair go?' that will be a sign that they need help."

"What should I do?"

"Step on your hydraulic lift, and do not stop the barber chair until you no longer see the child."

"Um." Logan hesitated as he looked at the barber chair. "I don't fully understand." He returned his gaze to the Angel, but he was gone.

Logan stepped to the area where the Heavenly being had been and started to doubt his encounter, except for the amazing feeling of peace that lingered.

A snore escaped Logan's lips, rousting him from his slumber. The bible he had been reading was on his chest. He closed it, setting it on the end table before raising the recliner. Logan ran his fingers through his slightly graying hair, then looked heavenward as he pondered the dream.

CHAPTER 1
The Faith Launcher

―∽∽―

Logan opened the joining door from his first-floor house to the two bedrooms that he converted into his barbershop. The oak floors were waxed, and everything was ready for the first day of the week.

Looking into the mirror, Logan combed his dark brown hair with spikes in front on his punkadour hairstyle, which was an updated version of the pompadour. A song burst from his lips. "Oh, Lord, it's hard to be humble when you're perfect in every way. I can't wait to look in the mirror. I get better looking each day!"

Logan paused and grinned as he stared into the brown eyes reflecting in the mirror. He winked and whistled the rest of the song while straightening up the barber tools.

The sun was streaming through the slats of the bamboo blinds on the east-side picture window. It promised to be another gorgeous day in the small farming community of Shelley, Idaho.

A car pulled up, so Logan raised the curtain, opened the separate entrance on the north side of his house, and motioned for the people to come in. He turned on the lights to begin another day.

Soon a mother whose eyes were bloodshot and surrounded by dark circles pulled her fourteen-year-old son through the door, who was dragging his feet.

"I hate to do this to you, Mr. Payne, but could I pick him up in thirty minutes?" Mrs. Butterfinkle asked. "His last day of school was yesterday, and Brady and Brooke don't get out until tomorrow. I need to run to their school for preparations on their Awards Banquet tonight."

"We'll be fine, won't we, Boone?" He placed his hand on Boone's shoulder.

Boone, who stood just four inches below Logan's six feet two inches, tore away from Logan and shoved his mother.

"Hey!" Logan raised his eyebrows as he stared at Boone. "Respect your mother, please."

Boone looked at Logan and decided not to test him. He plopped on one of the black vinyl chairs and loudly tapped his right foot.

"I'll be right back." Logan rested his hand under Mrs. Butterfinkle's elbow, escorted her out the door, and followed her to her car. "Is everything all right, Betsey?"

"Oh," she tried to smooth her tousled brown hair. "I must look a sight. Things have been a bit crazy with my husband away at work."

"Yes, I remember Jason's job requires him to be gone for long periods of time. Is there anything I can do?"

"No." She looked down with tears in her eyes. "I think we will be all right. Boone's been acting up and was suspended from school the other day."

"Yes, I noticed a little aggressiveness on his part."

"He's been bullying timid kids." Betsey's voice cracked. "My other two don't pick on him. Jason tries to spend time with him when he's home. I don't know what to do."

Logan touched her shoulder. "I'll try to talk to him if you'd like."

Betsey hesitated, and then said, "Yes, would you please?"

"You can count on it."

"You better get in there." Betsey pointed to his shop. "Boone's spinning around in your barber chair."

"I'll call you tonight and let you know what he said." Logan scurried to the barbershop and found Boone spinning fast enough that the chair was wobbling. He grabbed hold of the back and latched on to Boone's shirt to keep him from flying out of the chair.

"What a ride! How high does this chair go?"

Logan tilted his head and wondered if his dream was an actual visitation from an Angel. He looked at his schedule and saw no appointments booked for an hour and a half.

"It can go pretty high."

"Will you show me how high?" Boone's foot wildly tapped.

"Can you promise to sit still through your haircut?"

"I can do that!" Boone slid to the back of the chair.

"Okay." Logan placed a strip around his neck, and then a royal blue chair cloth. Boone shifted back and forth, and then settled in.

"I'm ready!"

Logan placed his foot on the hydraulic lever and watched the chair rise. It hesitated where it normally stopped and then continued on. Logan swallowed hard.

"Wow!" Boone looked down. "How much farther?"

"Um, you'll see." As the chair hoisted closer to the ceiling, Logan prayed under his breath, "Oh, Lord, let Boone be safe."

The ceiling turned translucent before it swirled causing the sound of rushing wind. Logan and Boone watched in stunned awe.

"Wait, stop!" Boone scooted down into the chair. "This is high enough!"

Logan looked outside and prayed that no one would pass. Boone screamed as the top of the chair hit the ceiling, and then stopped screaming when the ceiling expanded upward. Logan placed his hand on his chest trying to stay calm. As soon as the bottom of the chair cleared the top of the ceiling, the chair disappeared as if the ceiling gulped it whole. Logan released the lift and circled the chair as his pulse raced. He took deep breaths, trying to still his anxious heart.

The chair slowly returned to the floor…without Boone.

"How am I going to explain this to Betsey?"

The Angel he had seen in his dream appeared in the waiting room. "No harm will come to him, Logan. Although the enemy will set traps to hinder him, this is an intense lesson from the Lord God to draw Boone out of a self-induced destructive path. Pray that his journey will be swift and sure." He smiled, nodded and disappeared.

Logan looked at the ceiling and then opened the door connecting to his house. The attic ladder was in the hallway. Logan pulled the string dangling from the ceiling and raced up the ladder.

He fumbled to find the attic light switch. The florescent light flickered then came to life. There was no change in the attic. Logan huffed in frustration, as he flicked the light off and returned to the barbershop. *Is this another dream?*

Regardless of his doubts, he sat in the waiting room, staring at the empty barber chair.

"This can't be real." Then finally believing that maybe it was, he prayed. "Whatever You have planned for Boone, do it quickly, Lord."

CHAPTER 2
Boone's World

As the ceiling expanded and formed a bubble around Boone, he stopped screaming, wondering what was next. A gentle mist touched his face and tightened the blonde ringlets of his overgrown hair as he went through layers of clouds. When the barber chair entered a small room, it slowed then stopped. Two metal doors parted in the middle.

Boone crouched behind the chair before the doors fully opened. He peeked around until something passed by — or was it a person? Then another some…*thing* went by. They looked half human and half machine. More of them passed without any acknowledgement of the elevator being there.

There were lockers to the right, so Boone rushed beside them. He watched as many varieties of the machine people went from one room into another. *This must be a school.* One of them slowed when he noticed Boone.

What am I doing? The elevator hides me much better. Boone turned and bounced off the belly of a broad machine-like man. A clamp-shaped hand vised Boone's shoulder making it painful to move. Boone looked into an unwelcoming face. Metal was grafted into his skin exposing a human nose and mouth, but his eyes were vacant, as if waiting for instruction. In the middle of his forehead was a blue light in the shape of an eye. Boone couldn't stop staring at it.

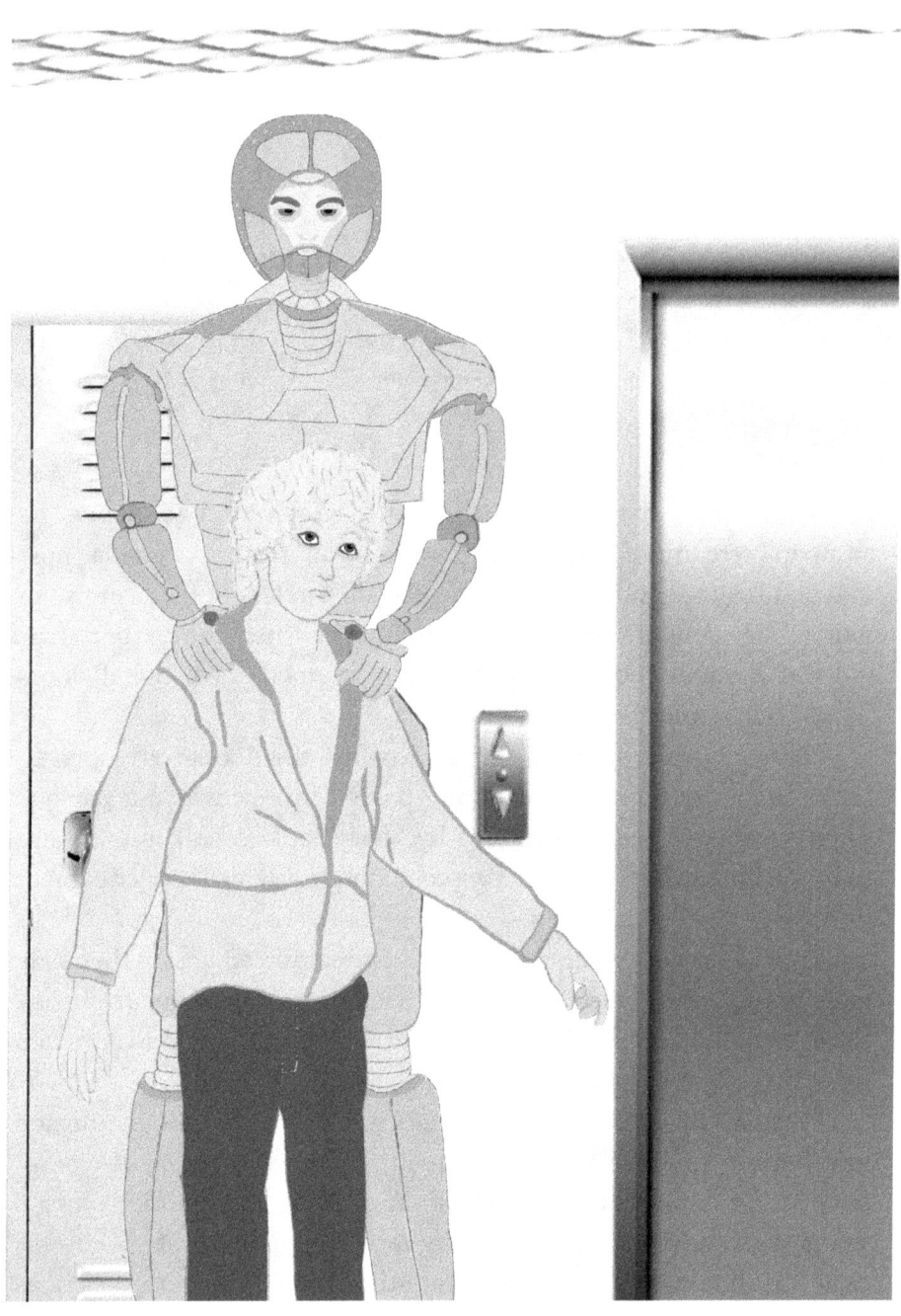

"Are you not Boone Butterfinkle?"

"How do you know my name?"

"We have been expecting you." The machine released his hold. "Follow me."

Boone watched the creature move stiffly toward a door on the other side of the hall. No one else was there, tempting Boone to run, until a hint of curiosity kicked in. *Ah, let's see what this is all about.*

They stood outside a glassed door and looked in.

"This will be your new classroom. I am the regulator, or what you call a principal here at MMS Freshman High. You may call me Mr. Regu."

"Why am I here?"

"You are here to be processed. Did they not tell you?"

"They? Who are they?" *On second thought…* "I need to go home now." He made a move to leave but didn't get far when Regu clamped his shoulder.

"You will stay," he said with no emotion. The robot opened the door and escorted Boone in.

All the machine children sitting at their metal desks turned their attention to Mr. Regu and Boone. Several children whispered and pointed at Boone until the teacher said in a higher computerized voice, "Children, this is our new Inductee, Boone Butterfinkle."

Snickers traveled from one end of the classroom to the other. Something like that would have normally ticked Boone off, but it sounded melodic in a computerized sort of way.

"Children! Remember how you were before you came here, and respect Boone's differences, please."

The teacher looked like a smaller version of Mr. Regu, only with curves. The eye in the middle of her head glowed green. She walked toward Boone, and he didn't realize that he had been holding his breath, which produced black spots in front of his eyes. Before Boone knew it, his knees gave way.

Boone could hear voices from a distance and tried to listen to what was being said, but only heard his heart beating in his ears. He opened his eyes and found everyone in the room standing over him. He rose quickly until things became black again.

"Stay there," a different computer-generated voice said. This robot wore a medic's cap on her head, and the color of her extra eye was purple. The children hovering over him didn't have the third eye, just an indentation where one could go.

"Mr. Regu, would you please take Boone to the nursing station?"

He knelt down and lifted Boone's 165-pound bulk like he weighed nothing. Boone leaned forward, trying to jump, until Regu squeezed his arms of steel tight enough that it impeded Boone's ease of breathing. They went to the end of the hall and turned left down a darkened foyer. Boone searched the dimly lit area for a chance to make a break should the Regulator lighten his grip.

This principal makes my principal seem like a wimp.

The nurse opened the last door in the hall to a room that smelled strongly of disinfectant. Boone squinted to the sudden brightness. There was a hammock across the room where Regu lowered Boone.

"Do not move." His voice was stern.

Boone complied until he saw the nurse approaching with a needle attached to a syringe the size of a round toothpick.

The nurses came alongside of Mr. Regu. "Hold still, boy."

"You're not coming near me with that!"

Mr. Regu placed a hand on Boone's shoulder and the other on his chest. That didn't stop Boone from thrashing his legs. The Regulator scooted down and laid his massive leg on top of Boone's.

It was a rare occasion when Boone couldn't boast about his strength. He was no match for this machine.

When the nurse lowered the needle into Boone's left wrist, a slight burning sensation flowed up his arm. Soon after his vision blurred.

"Someone help," a garbled plea escaped Boone's lips before the lights went out.

CHAPTER 3
Robotic Assembly

"Hey, kid." Boone heard a loud whisper in a hollow room. "Psst, wake up."

Boone's right leg throbbed as he moved on a hard cot.

"I need to ask some questions before they come back."

"Where am I?" Boone asked groggily.

"We're in a rehab installation."

"Why rehab?" Boone sat and shrieked when he saw his foot to his knee. It was encased in some sort of metallic material. Rivets connected from a silver foot to his ankle. Bronze and silver sheets curved in three-by-five-inch sections from his ankle to his knee, which also moved with the assistance of rivets.

"Quiet!" the boy said. "You don't want them to come back this soon."

Boone tried to stifle a sob. "What did they do to me?"

"Welcome to your worse nightmare."

The lights cast a red hue in the room. They were in a holding chamber with steel bars. Ten cots lined the length of the cell with only Boone and this boy.

"What's going on? I just went to get a haircut, and now I'm in this place!"

"Please," the boy begged in a loud whisper. "If not for yourself, for me, please keep your voice down!"

Boone tried to snuff up the mucus forming in his nose, and then decided to wipe it with the bottom of his West 49 t-shirt. "So what is this place?" Boone spoke softly, broken.

"Were you a bully on Earth?" the boy brushed away a piece of blonde hair that had fallen in his face. The kid was the same height as Boone, only not as bulky and had both legs up to his hip robotically adjusted.

Boone hesitated and then said defensively, "Yeah, so what of it?"

"I was too," the boy confessed. "And so was the other kid they just took."

"What's your name?" His bunkmate's green eyes were bloodshot, filled with fear and concern.

"Taylor Twitterbum."

Boone snorted. "I thought my name was bad."

"What's yours?"

"Boone Butterfinkle."

"Maybe it's our names…"

"What's the other kid's name?" Boone asked.

"Sawyer Scuttlegut.

"You're kidding me, right?"

"Nope. We thought it's because we're both bullies, but with your name, maybe it's our names that brought us here. I haven't met any other kids that have been assimilated to know what their names are, or if they're bullies."

The sound of a metal door opened to the main entrance, and both of the boys' heads snapped to attention. Taylor settled into his cot and whispered, "Act like you are sleeping. Sometimes they don't take you if you are sleeping."

Boone imitated Taylor and tried to relax his breathing. The cell door squalled, and the sound of two robots shuffling in chilled Boone to the core. It took Boone considerable effort to steady his breathing. Behind his eyelids, he detected a shadow beside him, and then he heard them plop someone in the cot between Taylor and him.

"He is sleeping," the robot said.

"This one, as well."

The cell door closed, and Boone waited for the sound of the entrance door closing before he opened his eyes.

Taylor didn't hesitate when all was quiet. He swung his robotic legs over the side of his cot and rushed to the boy's side.

"Oh, good, they didn't work on his head."

Boone stood on the other side of the boy. "Is that Sawyer?"

"Yep. They went to his neck." Taylor pointed to the new section. "The next surgery will be his arms, and after they work on his head, he'll have no memory of who he really is. When they're totally finished, we call them humbots."

Sawyer was at least six feet two inches and had fairly defined muscles in his arms. The chest plate that was attached was sterling silver and formed a perfect six-pack waist. His hair was red, cut short but flowed forward and spiked in front. That color of hair, combined with a generous sprinkling of freckles, was probably what destined Sawyer to be a bully.

"How long has Sawyer been here to get this far in the process?"

"He's been here three weeks. I've been here a week. When Sawyer got here, he watched three other kids go through this. Acting like he was asleep didn't save him last time. They took him anyway."

"We've got to find a way out of here."

"Good luck with that," Taylor said. "Sawyer heard some robots talking before the last procedure, about a boy and girl getting out of the cell. They hid in what they thought was an empty room, and Sawyer didn't fully understand what they did to them after they found them, but it didn't sound good. There are hidden cameras everywhere."

"Does that mean they're listening to us now?"

"There was another brainy bully locked in here with us. He looked over the cells pretty thoroughly and said he didn't think we are being monitored. Especially since they think we're sleeping, and we're not."

"You can give up escaping, but I'm not going to stay here to be turned into that." Boone pointed at Sawyer.

They heard the suction being released on the entry door and dove back to their cots. Taylor missed and fell onto the floor. Boone snuggled into his bed and closed his eyes. The humbots came in and moved quickly to Taylor.

"Leave me alone." Taylor tried to twist out of one robot's hold, but found himself in the arms of the other. "I don't want to go. I like how I am."

"We must remove the hostile part of you."

"I can quit being mean," Taylor cried. "Let me go!" He wrenched in every direction.

"Your educators tried several methods to end your bullying," the robot stated. "When you did not stop, they contacted us."

As soon as it was quiet, Boone wiped his tears. He couldn't believe the schools were in cahoots with this bully asylum. Sure, he roughed up one computer genius and had made a few bad choices, but he could stop anytime he wanted to. If Brianne Watchler hadn't brushed him off, he wouldn't be in this mess. She was the sweetest computer nerd he had ever seen.

Sawyer moaned and tried to move, which caused more groaning.

Boone hustled over to Sawyer and brushed his hand over his head. "Hey, dude, you're all good. They didn't adjust your head."

Sawyer's bloodshot eyes barely opened as he tried to bring this new person into focus. He pushed Boone away and asked, "Who are you?"

"Hey, chill. I'm in the same bad spot you're in."

"Not another kid."

"Boone Butterfinkle, at your service."

Sawyer snorted. "Don't make me laugh, it hurts. Is that your name for real?"

"Do you think I'd make a name like that up?"

"I thought Taylor's name was bad."

"Look who's talking, Mr. Scuttlegut."

Sawyer looked away without answering.

"You guys can't give up on trying to escape. No one's going to make me into some kind of a robot."

"You're not the first to say that, Boone, and probably not the last. Every one of us has been trying to escape. I don't think we want to know what they do to the ones who try and get caught."

"It can't be worse than being computerized to the point where you don't know who you are anymore."

"I need to sleep. When you come up with a plan, let us know."

Boone walked around the perimeter of the cell and looked for any inconsistency in the bars. There were a few welds that appeared weak. On the other side of the cell gate, a three-foot square vent on the wall came up to his knees. He strained to hear anything coming from the vent, hoping it connected all over the complex. A mild clanging drummed in a steady beat. Maybe it was the air-conditioning duct.

The electronic release on the entrance door made Boone fly to the top of his cot. The flimsy bed collapsed from the impact. Boone huddled to the corner of the cage as two humbots unlocked the cell. They didn't have Taylor with them.

"You can just forget it, dumbots," Boone warned. "I'm not going anywhere."

"You have no option."

They approached Boone from both sides. Boone sprang and kicked the closest robot in the crotch. Surprisingly, he went down. When the other humbot tried to grab Boone, Boone jabbed his fingers into his eyes. Boone couldn't believe how easy it was to incapacitate them. He dashed through the cell door and raced to the entry. Boone yanked open the door and ran chest first into three guards.

One seized Boone's arm and spun him around with his back against the guard's chest, then the android wrapped his arms around Boone and squeezed. Boone flailed his legs until the humbot took away Boone's ability to breathe.

"This one will be trouble." Boone heard his keeper say as he passed out.

CHAPTER 4
Remembering

The lights above Boone were so bright he could barely focus. He wanted to move but he couldn't lift his arms or legs. He looked away from the light and saw three humans standing over a table with surgical instruments.

"This one is becoming a problem already." He heard a female say.

"Yes, the Directive has ordered a quick revamping," the man said. "It will have to wait. We are backlogged."

"We've never had such a transference of bullies," another man said. "I wonder what's happening on Earth to create such an increase of hostile behavior."

"They are the lucky ones to be placed in our facilities. All memory is erased, and they are obedient to the Directive. They will be use for the greater good."

"I want to go home," Boone muttered.

The female ordered, "Give him more sedatives before we begin."

"I'll be good," Boone slurred. "Let me go home."

"It will be over in a minute."

"He's coming around."

"Why did they have to shackle him?"

"You didn't see the damage he did to the cell and the humbots."

Boone opened his eyes and saw the blurred outlines of Sawyer and Taylor. "Oh, my right leg hurts."

"Easy, Boone." Taylor patted his shoulder.

Boone tried to raise his arms to his head and stopped when restraints tightened. His eyes widened. "Get these things off of me!" He rattled the chains that went from wrist to wrist and down to his ankles.

"Calm down, Boone." Sawyer shoved him into the cot. "You're only making it worse."

"This is a nightmare!" Boone sank into his bed and turned his head as the tears flowed.

Sawyer motioned to Taylor to leave him alone. Boone heard them whispering back and forth, but he didn't care to listen because memories of the things he had done to kids at school invaded his thoughts.

He may have been suspended for the first time at school, but the terrorizing had been going on a lot longer. It started when Boone's dad didn't come home for his thirteenth birthday, like he had promised. His dad was stuck across the country due to a freak snowstorm. There was no flight home until after his March 8th birthday.

His mother, tried to make it a special day by inviting Boone's friends over, but turning thirteen was a big event. He wanted his father to be there for the rite of passage of leaving childhood and becoming a teenager. Being repeatedly disappointed, his adolescence took an unpleasant turn.

The next day at school, he found a lower classmate in the bathroom. The boy was severely ADHD and kept to himself most of the time. On the bathroom counter, Boone saw a report that was due that day. With the kid in a stall, Boone read it out loud in a childish tone. The boy burst out of the stall to retrieve his report, but Boone tore it in half, crumpled it and flushed it down a toilet.

The boy stammered, "I worked a month on that!" and stormed out. Boone heard later that the boy's mother printed another copy and delivered it to class in time. No one reported his first act.

The next time, he shoved the head of a computer nerd into a toilet when he wouldn't give Boone the dessert the kid's mother had packed. His victim listened to Boone's threat and didn't tell anyone.

More time passed, and Jason's continual broken promises fueled Boone's rage. He watched how the disabled children or computer nerds had the support of their fathers and targeted them to unleash that fury.

That self-turmoil motivated Boone to spend hours working out on weights and run rigorous treks to ease his heartbreak. In the process, his body became solid muscle.

Boone's dimpled cheeks and strong jawline made him a natural attraction for any girl. However, lifelessness reflected from his cold blue eyes, which made most girls hesitant to approach him, and those who ignored that sign of inner conflict quickly learned that he had no respect toward the opposite sex. Most of his own teammates steered clear of him, too.

It was only after his involvement with Brianne Watchler that he found himself in trouble. If only he hadn't been late handing in a science assignment. Mr. Harrison's solution to Boone's laziness was to pair Brianne and Boone on a science fair project.

Boone was one of the few freshmen who played at the varsity level on Shelley's football team and didn't pay any attention to Brianne because she was a computer geek. She used hot-pink rubber bands on her braces to match her large hot-pink glasses. When Brianne smiled, it was an overload of Boone's least favorite color. It looked like she rarely brushed her hair because the ends stuck out everywhere from the ball she attempted to style in the back of her head. Boone rarely saw her dressed in anything but a baggy t-shirt and worn-out jeans.

When they started the project, Boone's attention was never there. Brianne organized the assignment without his input. He had to admit that it was a pretty cool project. Brianne titled the experiment *Veggie Gases*.

Brianne wanted to find out which way vegetables created the most gas: fresh, canned or frozen after grinding each kind, and then placing them in a two-liter bottle containing two cups of vinegar, which sat for thirty minutes, and then added a quarter cup of baking soda. They placed a balloon over the bottles to test the amount of gas captured. So far, the preservative of salt in the canned carrots, beans, and corn caused a greater gaseous reaction than the fresh or frozen. They decided to save the peas for Friday's Science Fair.

Boone was invited to Brianne's house Thursday night to help pick the fresh peas.

Brianne's mom, Kim, a petite woman with a warm smile, charm and beauty, answered the door. Boone wondered why Brianne was such a geek when her mom was a babe for an older lady. Brianne's gene pool must have run on her father side.

Kim showed Boone to the kitchen table. It wasn't normal for Brianne to keep him waiting. He took the can of peas from the table and tossed them in the air, catching it in as many positions as he could think: behind his back, over his head, and under his legs.

"I wonder if that will taint our experiment," Brianne said as she looked at Boone turned upside down, looking through his legs.

In that position, Boone thought it must be her older sister talking to him, because it didn't look like Brianne. He straightened and turned around. His jaw dropped. Brianne's strawberry blonde hair flowed softly over her shoulders. Her glasses were replaced by contacts and there were no more braces. She wore a purple flower sundress that accentuated a figure that he never knew existed beneath the baggy clothes she usual wore. Brianne's green eyes sparkled when she smiled, exposing indentations on her cheeks.

"Uh, me—I do no harm...uh...to da peas," Boone stammered. His hands went to his eyes as shook his head. Boone blushed and smiled. "What happened?"

"What ever do you mean?" Brianne smirked with enjoyment of making the jock Boone Butterfinkle lose his composure.

"Where's the geeky Brianne Watchler? And you know exactly what I mean."

Brianne's dad, Stewart entered the kitchen and stopped abruptly when he saw how Brianne captivated Boone's attention. He ran his hands through his wavy blonde hair then yelled. "Kim get in here!"

"What?" Kim rushed in. "What's wrong?"

"Take her back. Take Brianne back and replace the anti-babe magnet we once had."

Kim looked at Boone's dazed expression. "Oh, we didn't think about that did we? Oh my."

Boone was far more attentive to Brianne than he ever thought he could be to any girl. Stewart hovered near as they picked the peas and shelled them. Then he escorted Boone to the door to make sure he left.

The next day at school, Boone was waiting for Brianne at her locker. There were many whistles and 'you go girl' comments as she walked through the school hall. Boone's lone buddy, Coffey Strong poked Boone in the rib and whispered, "Aw, dawg, I felt sorry for you when Harrison tied you to Brianne, but look at the geek now."

Boone shoved his athletic black friend away and approached Brianne.

"Hey, Brianne." Boone lifted her backpack off her shoulder so she could open her locker with ease. "Are you excited about the Science Fair?"

"Yes, it's my favorite time of the year."

"Once we win," Boone shuffled back and forth, "can we go to The Shake Shop to celebrate?"

"You mean like a date?"

"No, well, sort of."

"My parents won't let me date until I'm sixteen. That's two years away for both of us," she stated as she retrieved her notes from her locker, then slammed the door.

"It doesn't have to be a date."

"What changed?"

"What do you mean?"

"You know what I mean." Brianne grabbed her backpack from him.

"I, uh." Color rose to Boone's cheeks. "You look different."

"Exactly. That's a pretty lame reason to want to be around me now when I am essentially the same person I was Thursday morning when you called me *four eyes*."

"You tell 'im, Bree," said Laree, one of Brianne's closest friends. A crowd was forming now.

"You can't fault a guy for being an idiot, can you?"

"We're stuck together for this science project, then we can go back to the way it was before, where you didn't know I existed, except to occasionally torment me."

"Ouch!" Coffey said from the back rows of students circling the two.

Brianne walked through the crowded hallway headed toward the bus that was loading for the Science Fair. The children dispersed, and Coffey stood next to Boone.

"She'll go out with me, you just watch."

Boone should have left it there, but instead he devised a way to get her attention at the Science Fair. He weakened the balloon for the canned peas' two-liter bottle test by pricking the top layer.

Display tables were lined one after another. There were fifteen contestants from the ninth grade of the Shelley Russets, but a total of eighty-five from all schools in the Idaho Falls area. Boone and Brianne were in the back of the gymnasium, and one of the last pairs to demonstrate their project.

They gauged the extension of the balloon for the fresh and frozen peas, then Boone handed Brianne the doctored balloon for the canned peas bottle. Boone backed out of the area and found Coffey.

"Watch this," Boone said with a snicker.

"What have you done now?"

Seconds later, the weakened balloon exploded, covering Brianne from head to toe with foul pureed peas and vinegar. Mr. Harrison and three other judges, who were standing across the table from Brianne, also received a generous shower.

"As you can tell," Brianne said with pea paste sliding down her face. "The gases from the canned peas far exceeded the frozen and the fresh versions of the pea test. We determined that the preservatives in the canned products increased the gaseous state of the..."

No one could prove it was more than just a fluke. However, Brianne noticed Boone huddled near Coffey, laughing.

Boone continued to conveniently find himself in Brianne's path. Brianne signed up for the Memorial Day choir ensemble. Only five boys and five girls were going to be selected, so the twenty students who entered had to audition. Boone didn't know if he could sing, but he decided to audition with *America* for his piece.

Brianne was wearing a floral V-neck dress that flowed out just below her knees. She confidently walked to the microphone and placed it in hand. Coffey sat next to Boone and watched as a dazed grin appeared upon Boone's face.

"Man, dude, you have it so bad," Coffey whispered.

Boone didn't even hear him. The accompaniment had already begun, and Brianne's low alto voice danced through the auditorium. *God Bless America* had never sounded so sweet.

Five auditions later, it was Boone's turn. The music began, and Boone jumped in one bar ahead of time, off tempo, off key, and just plain off. He didn't even get to the second line before the kids booed him off stage.

"Don't sit by me, dude," Coffey said when Boone returned. "I cannot believe that one person can sing that bad."

Boone punched him and sat. "She'll go out with me, you just wait."

"Don't go serenading the girl, or you'll lose her for sure. I'm gonna have to re-evaluate our friendship." Coffey continued to talk, but Boone didn't notice. He was already scheming his next ploy to win Brianne's heart.

There was the end-of-the-year freshman dance. Each girl held ten tickets apiece as a fundraiser for their class. It cost two dollars a ticket to dance. The tickets were held in the principal's office, and the girl wouldn't know who bought her tickets until the dance.

Boone made a beeline to the principal's office to buy all of Brianne's tickets. Only one was left. Boone bought that ticket, and then started hunting for the other ticket holders.

When he approached five of his football chums, including Coffey, they all put their hands behind their backs or in their pockets.

"Hey Boones," J.J. said. He was an oversized teddy bear who played fiercely on the field, but was gentle as a lamb to everyone he knew. He towered over Boone, grabbed him, and messed his hair. "What's doing?"

Boone broke from J.J.'s grasp and shook his head to get his curls to fall in random organization. As a quarterback, Boone was no match for this oversized defensive tackle.

"There was only one ticket left of Brianne's. Do you guys know anyone else who bought her tickets?"

"Sorry, Boone," J.J. handed his ticket and left. "I didn't mean to move in on your girl."

Danny, a five-foot-five wide receiver stepped behind the guys and said, "Later."

"What gives you the right to own Brianne?" asked the team's middle linebacker as he approached the group. Even with Boone's impeccable features, Remmie was the best looking ninth grader in school. He was six foot tall, 175 pounds, and could bench press 180 pounds. His confidence sickened Boone, but the girls flocked to him. "I have two tickets, and you don't get them, so don't ask."

The group dispersed leaving Boone and Coffey behind. Coffey removed his hand from his pocket and produced a ticket. "Here, homey, I got you a ticket."

Boone gave Coffey an accusing look. "You too, Coffey?"

"No way." Coffey danced around Boone. "I was in line when I heard several guys buying tickets for Brianne, and I figured I better get one before they were gone."

"So you know who the other boys were?"

"Some, yeah."

"And..." Boone encouraged. Coffey didn't respond. "Who were they, dude?"

"One was her geeky friend, what's his name?"

"Dexter?"

"Yeah, that's the dude."

"Okay, I'll start with him." Boone walked toward the math lab where Dexter usually hung out.

CHAPTER 5

Regretting

It was the last period of the day and Boone raced out of his history class so that he could follow Dexter home.

Dexter's stature of ninety-pounds at four-foot-ten made him a target for bullying. He wore tight jeans that ended just above his ankles accentuating his white socks, and dirty Pro-Keds Asteroids. His greasy hair parted down the middle and flared over his large ears, which made them bend. Dexter walked with his head down and his hands in his pockets.

Boone followed him east on Fir Street and left on Lincoln where the irrigation ditches ran along the east side of the road. That's where he made his move.

"Hey, Dexter, what's up?" Boone came alongside and wrapped his arm around his shoulder.

Dexter scooted out of Boone's hold. "You never talk to me. What do you want?"

"I heard you bought something I want from you."

Dexter scrunched up his face and slid his large glasses up his nose. "When have you ever wanted anything I have?"

"When you bought Brianne's dance ticket."

Dexter stopped walking and looked at Boone. "It's not for sale. Not for a gazillion dollars."

"Look, geek." Boone grabbed the back of his neck and hauled him up the canal bank to a small overpass.

"Leave me alone, you dumb jock!"

Boone hoisted Dex by the back of his jeans and held him over the canal.

"Are you going to give the ticket to me?"

"No!"

For a little dweeb, Boone was impressed with his tenacity. Boone raised him higher and let loose enough to make Dexter think he let go, and then lifted him again.

"I can't swim, loser. You drop me and the ticket goes with me."

Something inside Boone snapped when he heard Dexter call him *loser*. He yanked Dexter onto the overpass, grasped the scrawny kid's hair and held him over the water. Dexter reached for Boone's hands and pulled up so his hair wouldn't disconnect from his follicles.

"Okay, okay, you win! Let me go, you can have it."

Boone released him on the overpass, and Dexter reached for his head to soothe it.

"The ticket." Boone extended his hand.

"Yeah, yeah." Dexter jammed his hand into his pocket and handed Boone the ticket. Boone snatched it and started walking away, until Dexter gave this warning, "Wait 'til Remmie hears about this. He'll stomp you real good."

Boone stepped in front of Dexter and said more to himself than anyone else, "Oh what the heck." He shoved Dexter in the chest and watched him hit the water with a large splash.

Dexter surfaced spewing water from his mouth. "Help!"

"Stand up, you geek, it's not that deep." Boone turned and walked away.

He could still hear Dexter carrying on a block away. *That makes four tickets and six more to find. Things are definitely looking up.*

Boone walked to his locker the next morning and was greeted by Coffey.

"Hey, dude, did you hear what happened to Dexter Ralston?"

Boone's heart skipped a beat. "No, what?" he tried to sound casual.

"He's in the hospital in a coma. They found him in the Lincoln Street irrigation canal."

"What happened?"

"At first they thought he just fell in, but everyone knows that Dex is terrified of going near the canal because he can't swim." Coffey leaned against the locker next to Boone's. "Then the docs said it looked like someone tried to rip his hair out because they found blood on the top of his head. Do you know anything about it?"

"Me, no. Why would I know anything?"

"You asked me who bought Brianne's dance tickets, and I told you about Dex. You can tell me if you had anything to do with it."

"Thanks, chump." Boone shoved him. "Thanks for believing I could do such a thing." Boone walked off, head down and worried.

Boone didn't want to think about Dexter right now, so he focused on the dance. It was only seven days away, meaning he had to hustle to find the other tickets. To Boone's amazement, Danny, the wide receiver handed two tickets as they passed in the hallway.

"You wouldn't happen to know who else bought one?"

"I know Remmie bought two, and I think Brianne's computer buddies, Monte, Russell, and Dexter bought the others. Man, did you hear about Dexter?"

"Yeah." Boone winced at the mention of Dexter. "It's not good. Thanks, Danny, I have to go."

Boone headed for the bathroom and lost the food in his stomach. It was impossible to keep his mind off of Dexter when everyone in school was talking about him. Boone had helped the little dweeb go from nobody to somebody that everyone cared about.

During lunch hour he saw Russell and Monte sitting together, so he put his tray next to them. "Hi, guys, can I join you?" Boone didn't wait for them to answer.

The boys looked at each other and rolled their eyes. Both were about Dexter's size, but at least dressed in T-shirts and normal jeans like other kids.

"What do you want?" Russell nervously ran his fingers through his sandy-brown buzz cut.

"Why should I want anything? Can't I just sit and chat with you?"

Monte wrestled a piece of chicken out of his braces. "You've probably talked to us twice since kindergarten, usually to pounce on us."

"Me? I wouldn't hurt you guys."

"Yeah, right," both said at the same time.

"Okay, so I want something. Would you two like to make some easy money?"

"Not if it involves you." Russell glanced at Monte.

"It depends." Monte shrugged.

"I hear you both bought a dance ticket for Brianne. I'll give you four dollars each for those. You'll double your money."

"No way." Russell's back straightened. "Brianne's our friend. We won't sell her out to you."

Boone's jaw tightened. "All right then, how about six dollars each?"

"Make it twenty dollars each, and we'll do it," Monte said, which got him a jab in his rib by Russell.

Boone shook his head. "Every geek has his price." Then opened his wallet. He had twelve dollars. "Okay, here's the deal. I'll have the twenty dollars tomorrow, and you have the tickets. Deal?"

"Twenty each, right?" Monte confirmed.

"Yep," Boone extended his hand into a fist, and both boys bumped to lock in the deal.

Boone wiped his hand and removed his tray from their table. He schemed the rest of the school hours on how to insure the forty dollars.

It was Boone's good fortune to get home thirty minutes before his older brother and sister. He knew where Brady's stash was and found fifteen dollars. Boone searched high and low in Brooke's room and came up empty. His parent's room was off limits, but he was desperate, so he entered the forbidden zone.

Boone hadn't been in their room since he was five-years-old, but it looked as he remembered. A huge bed with a sleigh head sat on the opposite wall of the entrance. He went to their dresser and started sliding out drawers. There was nothing. Boone went into the closet and turned on the light. Eight feet away he saw a shadow in the opposite wall. *Oh yeah.* There was a safe and the latch was down. Boone quickly knelt.

The sound of a car pulling into the driveway stopped him. Boone hung his head and backed out of the closet, turned off the light, checked to see if any drawers were open, and left the room. He ran downstairs, turned on the television, and jumped into the overstuffed recliner.

His mother came through the door and stopped by Boone. "When did you get interested in the cooking channel?"

"I heard they were running a series on cookie baking. I thought I'd check it out."

"Don't tell me you want to do the nutrition and foods class next year. Brooke wanted to do welding her freshman year, and now you want to cook. Where did Jason and I go wrong?" She continued talking to herself as she walked to the kitchen.

Boone followed her and sat at the table as she opened the refrigerator and pulled items to prepare dinner. Boone eyed her purse next to him.

"How was school today?" Betsey placed potatoes in the sink.

"Same as always. They're having the freshman-year-end dance next weekend."

"Oh, that's nice. Do you need any money?"

Boone rose and walked over to his mom. "Yes, actually. Could I have thirteen dollars?"

"Wow, is that enough? Seems like they were a couple of dollars per dance when Brady bought his tickets."

"Well, totally it would be twenty," Boone said.

Betsey wiped her hands on her apron and went to her purse. "Would you take out the garbage and mow the lawn?"

"Sure. Thanks, Mom." He reached over to kiss her on her cheek as he stuffed the twenty in his pocket. He gathered the garbage from every can in the house. On his way upstairs, he returned seven dollars to Brady's stash. *Things are turning out great.*

Boone was waiting for Monte and Russell by their lockers the next morning.

"Do you have the tickets?"

"Do you have the money?" Monte countered.

Boone showed the money, so each boy produced his ticket. They left for class, and Boone pulled out the other six tickets.

How would he get the two tickets from Remmie? He said not to even bother asking for them, but Boone wouldn't let that discourage him.

For a few seconds, Boone reflected on the fact that he didn't even give Dexter the option of getting money for his ticket. Monte and Russell were easily bought; maybe Dexter would have been too. Would Remmie do the same? It wouldn't hurt to try.

Boone saw Remmie pulling a book out of his locker.

"Hey, Remmie."

"Hey Boonester, what's up?"

"You said you have two of Brianne's dance tickets. Would you be willing to part with them if you made a little money?" Boone looked into Remmie's dark brown eyes, trying not to be intimidated by his height and confidence.

"Oh, I thought it was a rumor.

"What?"

"I heard that you're convincing the others to part with her tickets." Remmie started for his class, so Boone followed.

"People are talking about it?"

"Yeah. If I've heard, then Brianne's probably heard too."

"It shouldn't matter if she knows."

"Can I think on it, Boone?" Remmie stopped at the door of his math class. "She's the kind of girl that I'd like to get to know."

Boone tried not to look disappointed. "Sure, it's totally up to you."

"You got that right." Remmie entered his classroom.

The second bell rang and Boone realized he was late for his computer class again. When he entered just at the last bell, Mr. Gottschalk frowned at him. "Find your seat, Boone. We have a quiz this morning."

Boone scanned the room for Brianne, but she wasn't there for the second day in a row. That wasn't like her. He would have to do some investigating to find out what was going on.

The quiz was a struggle since Boone couldn't focus on the test. He wasn't sure if he passed it, but wasn't really concerned about it.

Monte and Russell were standing near the drinking fountain.

"Would either of you know where Brianne's been for the last two days?"

Monte and Russell exchanged looks. Russell wiped his mouth. "She's been at the hospital, reading Dexter his assignments."

Boone stepped back as if one of them had struck him. "Did he come out his coma?"

"Are you okay?" Monte asked. "You look sick."

"Yeah, I'm fine." Boone tried to regain his composure.

"Dexter and Brianne have been the best of buds since they were kids," Russell said. "No, he's still in a coma, but the nurses say that type of stimulation is good for him. Brianne's really worried about him. She reads his homework to him and goes home at night to do her own."

"Wow, that's," Boone couldn't find the words. "That's really something. Thanks. I'll talk to you later."

Boone's legs felt like lead. He tried to move quickly to the boy's restroom, but found it hard to breathe. Boone was relieved that no one was there. He barely made it to a toilet before throwing up.

When Boone focused on other things, he was able to ignore what he had done. But everywhere he turned, someone was talking about Dexter. Boone tried to convince himself it didn't matter, but his body wasn't listening.

"Boone, wake up," Sawyer shook him. "You're dreaming."

Boone opened his eyes and remembered he was living a different nightmare where teens were turned into robots.

"You were weeping, dude. Do you need to talk about it?"

"I deserve to be here, Sawyer." Boone wiped his nose with his shirt. "There's a boy who's in the hospital because of me, and he's in a coma."

"We've all done things we regret. That's why we're here, I guess."

"Did they take Taylor?"

Sawyer nodded.

"Who's that?" Boone pointed at the boy several cots over.

"I don't know. He hasn't woken up yet. They also brought two girls in the other cage. They took one of them away after they delivered this kid in here." Sawyer motioned behind them. "That's not good for them, but it is for us."

"What do you mean?"

"They'll work on them before they move on to us. They try to transform each person in the first two stages quickly, so it keeps us off guard. They are having trouble keeping up with new arrivals."

"Oh, I remember hearing the doctors talk about that before my operation."

"Try to get some rest, Boone. It's the only real rest you'll get for a while."

"Thanks, Sawyer." Boone rolled over. It was difficult finding a comfortable position with shackles on, but Boone was soon asleep.

CHAPTER 6
Suspension

It was the night of the dance so Boone pressed his best jeans and wore a sateen Scully Wahmaker shirt, on which a panel of the fabric was buttoned in a rectangular shape in the front. The royal blue color of the shirt made Boone's eyes even more crystal. His two-tone boots with rust and dark brown were shined to the max. Boone swept his longer sides around his ears and allowed his natural curls to wave freely on top.

When Boone entered the school cafeteria, he hardly recognized it. The tables were gone with chairs lining the walls and several decorations hanging throughout.

Coffey had to take a second glance at his best friend. "Whoa, dude." Coffey approached him with a smile. "I've never seen you look so sick!"

Boone slid his hand across Coffey's palm, then pointed his index finger at him. "You're looking smazing yourself, bro. Have you seen Brianne?"

"Nope, not yet."

"How about Remmie?" Boone scanned the room. "Oh, I see him. I'll talk to you later, Coffey."

Remmie was talking to Laree, so Boone interrupted and asked if Remmie would help move more chairs to the dance area. Remmie excused himself and followed Boone out to the hall and down the corridor to another hallway.

"Why do we need more chairs? It looks like they have enough." Remmie said as they turned opposite of the library. Boone unlocked a door to another hallway.

"They've counted the tickets sold and say they don't have enough." Boone bit his lower lip.

He roved his eyes over Remmie and was surprised how casual he dressed. The jeans he wore were faded. He had on a white shirt with red stripes that Boone had seen him wear to school several times. The dude was either way overconfident or had no idea how much chicks liked guys to dress up.

Boone unlocked another door. "Do you get the feeling they don't want us wandering back here? I mean, two locked doors in this hall."

"I can't believe they trusted you with a key," Remmie said.

Remmie wouldn't believe what Boone had to do to get a key.

"I've never been in this room." Remmie watched Boone open the door. "I've always wondered what was behind this metal scrolling window next to this door."

Boone motioned for Remmie to enter, and he did so eagerly. "A washing machine and dryer? Is that all?"

"The chairs are through that door in the back." Boone motioned him forward. Remmie went in, turned right and to the end of the room. Boone shut the door, locking Remmie in. *Dance number one and two will not be filled on Brianne's docket tonight.*

Remmie pounded on the door. "Butterfinkle, open this door now!"

Boone locked the second door and joyfully tossed the keys in the air. *The rest of the night belongs to me.*

The dance promptly started at 9 p.m. Boone eagerly watched for Brianne's arrival, but she didn't show for the first two dances. When Boone sat through two more dances, he paced the perimeter of the floor, trying to find Brianne. By the time dance number eight was announced, Boone's patience had run out. He thrust open the gymnasium doors with force and stomped to his dad's car. There was only one other place he knew she would be – the hospital.

Boone only had a learner's permit but talked his mom into letting him drive the mile to school in his dad's Ford Mustang. He peeled out of the parking lot and raced to Center Street, taking the back roads to Idaho Falls. Only Boone's lack of experience kept him from driving faster than he should. When Boone pulled into the Mountain View Hospital parking lot, he loosened the grip on the steering wheel because his hands were tingling.

The Watchler's coffee-colored Scion was parked seven rows away from the entry. Boone slammed his fist on the seat next to him. He didn't mean to seriously hurt Dexter, but Brianne's obsession to be by his side had to be stopped.

Fortunately they had parked in a dimly lit area. Boone pulled next to the Scion and rummaged through the glove compartment. He clutched a fingernail clipper before getting out of the car. Kneeling beside the passenger front tire of the Scion, Boone let the air out. Perhaps this would teach Brianne that she shouldn't be alone late at night.

After Boone turned on Sunnyside Road, he thought of other ways to teach Brianne not to ignore him. Red and blue lights behind him drew his attention away from his tirade. He glanced at the speed and was ten miles over the limit...without a proper license. He swore under his breath and slowed.

When Boone came to a stop, he slumped in the seat as he unrolled his window with the officer at his door. "Registration and license, please."

Boone pulled his license from his wallet and then grabbed the registration.

"I will be right back." The officer went to his vehicle. It wasn't long before he returned. He shined the flashlight in Boone's face and then said, "Would you please step out of the vehicle, son?"

Boone opened the door, and the officer escorted him to the back of the Mustang. "Place your hands on your vehicle and spread your legs."

"I'm not carrying anything, officer." Boone's voice was shaky.

"What are you doing in Idaho Falls this late with just a permit, son?" The officer patted him down. "You were going eleven miles over the speed limit. Are you in a hurry to get away from somewhere?"

The policeman spoke into his intercom. "This is IFPD 22 calling on the 510, is there anything further on the 484?"

"Car 22," the dispatch said. "The 484 has been apprehended."

"Roger that," the officer said. "I'm going to have to take you to the station, son. We'll impound your car. You can call your parents there."

Boone shook his head and grumbled, "You idiot, Boone…"

The officer opened the back door and Boone slid in. It was a long drive to the police station and an even longer wait for his mother to arrive.

Betsey walked to Boone and asked, "Are you all right?"

Boone nodded and looked away.

"We'll talk later. I have papers to fill out."

Boone watched her go to the counter. She looked so sad when she returned. "Come on."

The journey to the Toyota Rav 4 was uncomfortably quiet, and then Betsey turned to Boone. "Okay, let's have it."

"I don't want to talk about it."

"Well, that's not an option. I knew I shouldn't have let you drive the Mustang with just a permit. It's just - I know you're hurting with your dad being gone all the time. I wanted to make tonight special for you. You look so mature all dressed up. What happened? Did one of the kids at the dance persuade you to drive into town?"

"No. I just got angry, and before I knew it I was in Idaho Falls."

"So that's why you weren't paying attention to how fast you were driving, because you were angry? Why were you so angry?"

"It's stupid now."

"Exactly, Boone. It's stupid to be so angry that you can't even think straight enough to know you're breaking the law. I would ground you from driving until sixteen, but I won't get that chance because Bonneville county recommends that you can't even finish the driving course until after you turn sixteen."

Boone dropped his head into his hands and didn't move. Betsey started the car and drove home in silence.

Boone realized that Brianne probably had been driven to the hospital by one of her parents because she was too young to drive also. He just hoped this didn't get out, or someone would place him at the hospital parking lot.

———

Boone stayed in his room most of the weekend until Sunday afternoon. Officer Nutt was standing in the family room, waiting for Boone after his mother had summoned him downstairs. Brady and Brooke stopped watching television and listened to what was going on.

Officer Nutt had always been involved with his community throughout Boone's growing years. His slim build spread over a six-foot-one frame made him look pretty harmless until he put a uniform on. His shortly cropped gray hair created an appearance of authority, but his light blue eyes shined a kindness that could not be mistaken.

"I have a few questions for you, Boone," Officer Nutt began. "I know you know Remmie Christensen because you're both on the Shelley football team."

Boone's startled expression told Officer Nutt everything he needed to know.

"Remmie said you locked him into the storage room Friday night. The janitor just found him two hours ago. He is very hungry and dehydrated."

Betsey looked at Boone in disbelief. "Boone?"

"I — I didn't mean to leave him there. I forgot all about it."

"Well, that is unfortunate because his parents want to press charges."

Boone couldn't stop the tears. "Will he be all right?"

"He's recovering, but you have a mess to clean up. I see you had a little joy-ride to Idaho Falls that night, too, with just a permit."

"Is he under arrest, Mike?" Betsey asked.

"I'm taking him to the 3B Detention Center in Idaho Falls. He'll be booked, and he'll see a judge tomorrow. I'll give you a call in the morning when we know his appointment.

"This is a part of my job that I truly hate. Turn around, Boone, and hands behind your back."

Boone complied with the tears streaming and head down. He couldn't bear to see the disappointment on his family's faces.

"You really screwed up, son. This is a big warning for the path you're on."

"I know." Boone's voice softened as he swallowed a sob.

"You have the right to remain silent..."

Boone's mom approached him, put her arms around his neck and kissed his cheek. "I love you, Boone. We'll figure this out."

Boone looked into the eyes of total love and nodded as he moaned.

Monday morning at eight, the phone rang. It was Officer Nutt. "Boone is scheduled for ten in Judge Clark's chambers at the Blackfoot Courthouse. The good news is Remmie doesn't want to press charges, so his parents may drop them. Be there by 9:30."

"Okay, thank you, Mike."

"If there's anything I can do, just let me know."

Betsey grabbed her purse and headed for the garage but stopped when the phone rang. "This is Superintendent Foster. Mrs. Butterfinkle, do you have a moment?"

"Yes, what is it Mr. Foster?"

"I need to talk to you about Boone's recent activities at school, is there time today that you can drop by my office?"

"Yes, sometime this afternoon. I'm not sure when. I'm leaving for a meeting with Judge Clark in Blackfoot. I think after school gets out would be good."

"I have you down. We'll see you when you get here."

Betsey hung up and lowered her head to pray. "Dear Lord, be with us today. This is going to be a rough one."

—∿—

Betsey entered the outer chambers of Judge Clark's office and found Officer Nutt sitting with Boone.

"The Christensens are in the chamber right now. There's still a chance the charges will be dropped."

"How did you sleep last night, Boone? You look tired." Betsey wrapped her hand around his.

"It's a night I don't want to repeat."

"I didn't know you would be here, Mike."

"I had some free time this morning, so I thought I'd extend some support. I've watched Boone grow up from a baby. Sometimes we need a little help along the way to adulthood."

"I can't tell you how much we appreciate it."

"Mrs. Butterfinkle, Boone," the clerk said. "You may go in now."

Boone took a deep breath and followed his mother into the judge's chamber.

"Good luck, Boone," Mike said.

"Thank you."

The chamber was a scaled down model of a full-sized courtroom. Even after watching numerous law shows, Boone wasn't prepared for the foreboding he felt as he approached the judge.

"Honorable Ronald Clark presiding."

"Have a seat, Mrs. Butterfinkle and Boone." The judge's deep voice made the occasion all the more somber.

The man was as tall as Boone, but slightly overweight. He was graying at the temples and swept his hair back. Boone sought to read the man by looking into his eyes. They were brown and warm, but weary.

"This is your lucky day, young man. Remmie convinced his parents to drop the charges against you."

Boone exhaled the breath he was holding. Betsey smiled.

"I have listened to them express their concerns for the last fifteen minutes. If it was me, I would not have been so lenient.

"In one night you caused harm to Remmie and broke the law by driving illegally. If you come before this counsel one more time, I will administer the disciplines needed to help you understand the seriousness of your actions. Do you understand me, young man?"

"Yes, your Honor." Boone struggled to find his voice.

Would it be just a matter of time before they found out about him deflating Brianne's tire? And then there was Dexter.

"You may be excused."

The clerk ushered them out a door in the rear of the room. Boone and Betsey walked down the halls of the courthouse silently.

Boone spoke first when they were in the car. "I'm sorry, Mom."

"Your dad will be home the weekend after school is out. Let's sit down and talk about all this then. We have time for lunch and then we have an appointment to see the superintendent."

"Oh boy," Boone mumbled.

Somehow sitting before Superintendent Foster was more terrifying than Judge Clark. The man was of huge bulk and at least six-foot-four. Frown lines were ingrained in his face, and his eyes revealed his unhappiness. He folded his hands and stared at Boone.

"Young man, you are a real disappointment to Shelley High School. I don't even try to understand the pressures that children face today compared to when I was young, but I have never seen anyone go from no trouble-to-trouble that concerns everyone so quickly until last weekend.

"From what I understand, you have been all but stalking Brianne Watchler. That will end today, do you understand?"

"Yes, sir."

"The list of offenses raises a lot of concerns. Stealing school keys to lock Remmie where no one would find him for days, driving without a license, harassing Brianne and we suspect more..."

Boone shifted beneath his stare.

"It is the decision of our faculty that you are suspended effective immediately. You will take your last two tests at home. There are only three days left of school for the year, but your record will be filed, and they will decide next fall what measures of protection from the other children they will take. You will go into the sophomore year, but this record will follow you through high school."

Superintendent Foster's scowl turned to Betsey. "Mrs. Butterfinkle, when your husband gets back in town, you need to schedule an appointment with me to discuss this matter."

"Yes, sir. He'll be back the first weekend of June."

"We have cleaned out Boone's locker and stored it in the box behind you. Please, Boone, whatever is bothering you, you need to find someone to talk to. There are counselors in this district who you know. Schedule an appointment after school is out."

"Yes, sir."

"Good. You may be excused." The superintendent ushered them to the door.

Betsey didn't wait until they were alone, but spoke after the door was shut.

"Why were you stalking Brianne?"

"I just wanted to be friends and she wouldn't let me."

"Boone, what is going on? Do you realize how serious stalking someone is?" She didn't wait for Boone to answer. "I was stalked by a boy in college who wouldn't take no for an answer. When a girl says no, respect that!" Tears streamed down Betsey's face.

No more was said as they drove home. Boone jumped out of the car and dashed to his room. That is where he stayed until his mother roused him for a haircut, which guided him into a new nightmare.

CHAPTER 7
Planned Escape

The squeal of the door next to their cell woke Boone.

Sawyer and the new boy were watching the guards deliver a girl and take another. Her cries made Boone's chest tighten, especially after remembering how he made his mother cry.

"How are we going to comfort her from here when she wakes?" the new boy asked.

Sawyer's eyes moistened as he looked down. "It's amazing how planning ways to torment other kids has vanished since I got here."

"It changes when you're the one being picked on." Boone swung his legs off his cot. "Is it morning?"

"I have no clue what time it is or how many days I've been here. These humbots function twenty-four-seven."

"I'm Boone." He waved his shackled hands to the new teen.

"I'm Dallas." His grayish eyes showed fear then brightened. "Sawyer says you're working on a plan to get us out of here. I never thought I'd want to go home for anything, but after just a few hours here, I'm ready."

"What a sorry group we make," Sawyer said. "We pick on nerds to make ourselves feel better and end up here."

"That wasn't my issue. I got angry because my dad was always working and missed things I thought were important. I unleashed my anger on kids weaker than me."

"You have a dad?" Dallas said. "You're lucky. I never knew my father."

"I know my dad," Sawyer interjected, "but he won't have anything to do with me."

The girl in the other cell groaned and turned toward the boys. Sawyer and Dallas walked to the bars of the adjoining cells and waited for her to regain consciousness. They restlessly watched, wanting to help.

Her eyes fluttered, then opened wide when she remembered. She lurched out of her cot, but fell when the awareness of pain hit.

"Oh man." Sawyer leaned heavily against the bars causing them to sag. Boone quickly hobbled to Sawyer's side.

"But of course. I'm almost fully robotic. I'm way stronger than I used to be." He stepped away and pulled the two bars in opposite directions. They bent all the way to the next bars. Sawyer tried to squeeze through but was too bulky. He looked at Dallas but he patted his portly belly, and then asked Boone to try.

Boone jingled the shackles on his wrists. "Can you get these off, Superman?"

Sawyer smiled as he pulled the cuffs, and they separated. Boone rubbed his sore wrist and went through the bars.

"Keep your eyes and ears tuned to the entrance." Sawyer told Dallas.

As Boone approached the girl, she scooted across the floor to the cell door. "Leave me alone, don't come near me."

"I'm not here to hurt you, I'm just like you." Boone slowly advanced. "We don't want to be here either, so we're trying to stick together."

Her deep brown eyes searched Boone's, and then she looked at Sawyer and Dallas. Both boys nodded. "Oh," she spoke apprehensively. "Okay."

Boone picked up the girl and laid her on the cot. Her fear washed over Boone. "It's okay."

The girl looked athletic and medium in size, but with her short haircut, Boone gathered that she was a tomboy.

"Where am I? Who are you?"

"I'm Boone, and you're in a holding cell waiting to be robotized."

"How'd I get here and why?"

"I'm not sure how you got here, but why, well—are you a bully by chance?"

"I don't see what concern that is of yours."

"Well, I am, and so are my two friends. From what we've heard, it's our bad behavior they're trying to eliminate by making us more robot than human."

"Okay, so I've picked on a few kids in my school. How would they know about it here?"

"The schools contact this place somehow. What's your name?"

"Joy."

"That's Dallas and Sawyer." They waved.

"Boone," Sawyer whispered loudly. "You better get in our cell. Taylor's probably done with his procedure."

"We're right over here, and we can talk more through the bars, okay?" Boone squeezed through the bars.

Sawyer bent the bars back, and they returned to their cots.

"That means I'm next, doesn't it?"

Sawyer nodded. "Then me, and I won't remember you anymore."

"Then you need to make a move to escape while they're operating on me. How long does it take to do the hip surgery?"

"I'd guess around four hours."

"There's a vent over there." Boone pointed through the bars. "It sounds like it goes to some mechanical room. Take everyone out and go."

"But what about you?" Dallas asked.

"Now that I know you gain strength with each procedure, I'll join you and bring anyone new along."

"How will you know where we went?" Sawyer asked.

"Just send word through the vent."

All eyes turned to the entrance door when they heard the suction being released.

"Oh boy." Boone picked up his chains. "You need to put these back on."

Sawyer snapped the wrist portion in place but didn't get the ankles before the guards made it to the cell. Boone sank into his cot.

Two guards carried Taylor on a stretcher as another one opened the door. The robotics now covered Taylor's chest.

"It is your turn," the tallest humbot said, pointing at Boone. "Will you come peacefully?"

Boone stood and moved toward the door. The other guard pointed at his feet. "Your shackle is broken. I need to repair it." He bent to snap it together. It would have been so easy for Boone to smash in his face, but his friends had a plan to escape, and he wouldn't ruin it.

With one guard in front and the other behind, Boone shuffled along. It was the first time he willingly walked with them. It took everything inside him not to scream as his chains clanged against the concrete floor. He didn't know what he would find when he returned, but he truly hoped that his friends would find freedom.

CHAPTER 8

Capture

The rapid shaking of his cot rousted Boone out of his recovery time from the robotic transformation of his hips. Boone opened his eyes and wasn't welcomed by his friends. There were five humbots with machine guns dangling over their right shoulders. All of them had a midnight blue light flashing from their extra eye.

"Where have your cellmates gone?" the one standing in the middle asked. He had three gold stripes on each side of his helmet.

"In case you didn't notice, I just came out of surgery. How would I know where they are?"

"You talk between each other," the captain's voice droned. "Surely you knew they were planning an escape."

"Hey, if they left me, they're no friends of mine."

They turned and huddled to talk.

"There is no sign of the gate being unlatched, it must have been a malfunction," the humbot with two strips on his helmet spoke.

"More than likely, it is an inside job," another said.

"Impossible," the captain stated. "The revamping is so complete, there has never been a defection. How far along was Scuttlegut?"

The woman robot tapped on her watch. "The next procedure would have been his total revamping."

"We might be able to pick him up on the homing device," the captain said. "Let us go check this possibility out."

They filed out to the entrance gate. When they were gone, Boone tried to swivel out of the cot but was too sore. He rose up on his elbows and looked behind him. They were gone. Every one of them had escaped.

Boone lowered himself to his cot and squeezed his watery eyes shut. He just wanted to rest so that he could do what was needed to rejoin his friends.

———

The entrance gate unlatched so loudly in the quietness of the empty cells, it woke Boone from a deep slumber. Didn't he just close his eyes; why were they returning? He looked to see if a new bully was being delivered, but no such luck. Two guards with flashing midnight blue lights came into his cell.

Boone hadn't realized it earlier, but he no longer wore shackles. He must have passed the non-aggressive test.

"Up." A short guard tapped the end of his rifle into Boone's leg. "Get up."

"Okay, okay." He was surprised how good his hips felt. Maybe he rested longer than he thought. "It can't be time to be transformed again."

"Come with us," the guard swiftly moved forward.

"What's the big hurry?"

"Quiet, Butterfinkle," the short one said.

"I hope they give me some friendly computer chips when I'm totally revamped."

The guard behind thumped Boone's shoulder with his rifle.

"Okay." Boone picked up the pace. "I'll shut up."

They exited the cell chamber, and instead of taking a right to the surgery room, they turned left.

"Where are we going, fellas?"

They continued to the end of hall, and then down a stairwell that was dimly lit. The stairs were made out of stone blocks, and the walls became darker as they descended, smelling damp. It reminded Boone of the old castles he researched for a sixth grade report.

The stairway spiraled one direction, and then back the other. The temperature dropped to the point where all additional parts of his body began to ache. Finally they came to a large room at the bottom of the stairway. There were monitors covering every outside wall. The guards escorted Boone in front of the first monitor and shoved him into a chair. The captain turned around and stared at Boone.

"I am Captain Babs. We spoke earlier."

"I remember."

"We have brought you here to show you what happens to escapees." The captain turned on a monitor, and Boone gasped when Sawyer appeared. Wherever he was, it was void of life. A haze floated around Sawyer as he struggled to climb a rock wall.

The camera shifted to the ground below. Boone leaned forward in anticipation. A riverbed of blades, axes, spiked briars, and nails welcomed a horrid death should Sawyer fall. Several pit bulls were on both sides of the river, straining to be released from their guard.

Boone's heart thumped when Sawyer turned around. His face was so scabbed over from extreme heat that he was hardly recognizable.

"You may think that we are trying to harm your cellmate, but we are actually trying to capture him to save him. You see, the environment outside this cohabitation is hostile. If we do not get to Sawyer soon, he will die."

"Yeah right. You placed that bed of weapons below to show your love."

The guard from behind slapped Boone.

"Stand down!" Captain Babs scolded the humbot. "Forgive his impulse to strike. He is newly revamped."

Boone rubbed his face, eyeing the one who hit him. "What have you done with the others?"

'They have not been found. We hope they have not expired."

When Sawyer made it to the top of the wall, many guards greeted him. One of them moved behind Sawyer and squeezed the right side of his neck, causing Sawyer to collapse.

"You will remain here, and we will have you watch the procedure of Sawyer's total transformation. Sawyer will be the first to have recall of his former memory after the revamping. He will be our experiment. We need his memory intact to lead us to the other escapees." The captain turned to a guard. "Bind our guest to his chair, so we will not have to guard him."

Two guards wrapped Boone's arms to his chair with a fabric he had never seen before. He couldn't move an inch.

Wherever Sawyer was transported, it was televised. They loaded him into a mobile tent, and a platoon of ten guards carried him through terrain of boulders and remnants of trees that looked as if they had been snapped in two during a tornado. Not one bird or animal was seen, and only the sound of robotic motion could be heard from the speakers.

It was thirty minutes before the sign of bushes and trees came into view. A river that was so perfect it had to be manmade, circled a city that was encased in a glass bubble. The lower portion of the bubble sparked with a stream of voltage running through; obviously their protection from the outside and for confinement within. How Sawyer escaped was something Boone wanted to know, as well as his captors.

When they passed through the coded entrance, the monitor faded.

"They shall be with us soon." Captain Babs entered the room. "If we had not found him, he would have died within the hour. If the others are out there, they are long gone. We imprison you for your own safety until you are entirely processed."

Oh, come on, who does this guy think he's kidding? Boone closed his eyes to avoid upsetting the situation by his poor reaction.

"We will put you in a room with Sawyer so that you may help us find the others."

"And how am I supposed to do that?"

"You two were imprisoned for some time, and he most likely trusts you." The captain touched the fabric around Boone's arm, and they released. "Come."

Boone followed the captain as two guards followed him. They entered a small white room that smelled of antiseptic, with a bed in the corner and a chair next to it.

"Sit. Sawyer will be here soon."

They closed the door, and Boone looked for any signs of listening devices. He couldn't find any, but he knew they were going to be monitored somehow.

The door opened, and Boone rose when two large humbots carried Sawyer in. A nurse followed close behind. They lowered Sawyer to the bed, and the nurse handed Boone a tube of ointment.

"Put this on his face, it will heal him quickly." She actually sounded compassionate.

When they left, Boone stared at Sawyer's face. He no longer looked sixteen-years-old. His face was cracked like old leather; bleeding and blistered. Boone scooted his chair closer and placed the ointment on the clean rag that was set on the table. He dabbed the balm gently on to his friend's face. As hard as Boone tried to prevent it, tears kept filling his eyes.

Within five minutes, the swelling and redness decreased. Boone turned the tube toward him to read the ingredients, but it simply said *Healing Salve*. Another few minutes and Sawyer's eyes opened.

"Water, please." His was voice raspy.

The door opened, and the nurse returned with a container of water and two glasses, and then left the room. It confirmed Boone's suspicion that they were being watched.

Boone raised Sawyer's head and helped him drink. Sawyer gulped too quickly and coughed it up. Boone tried again, and Sawyer slowly sipped, then sank into the comfort of the bed. His eyes closed, and Boone could tell by his breathing that he was asleep. Boone dabbed more ointment on Sawyer's face. It seemed forever before Sawyer's eyes opened again.

Sawyer reached for the water and helped himself. "I didn't get too far, did I? Did they catch the others?"

"You're the only one." Boone looked intently into Sawyer's eyes, trying to warn him not to say too much.

"We split up. I thought we would be harder to catch. I couldn't believe how harsh the conditions were outside the perimeters. There's not enough oxygen to go very far. The heat's like walking in an oven. If the others are out there, they won't survive." Sawyer turned his head as the tears freely flowed.

Two guards entered the room and motioned for Boone to follow.

"I'll be seeing you, Sawyer." Boone hoped that was true.

When Boone returned to the cell, he couldn't believe how lonely he felt. He wondered if Sawyer was telling the truth about the others going outside the compound's bubble. Or were the others still hiding somewhere in the compound? He had to proceed as if they were.

While Boone dreaded that anyone else should be brought to this horrid nightmare, he longed for companionship. There was no way he could find the way home by himself. How could an organization get away with selecting a group of kids to conform to their idea of good? In a wild sort of way, Boone and his friends were now the ones who were being bullied by these cyborgs. What a turn of events!

Boone inhaled as he flew to his feet.

Wait a minute. I chose the computer whiz to pick on, and now the computers are after me. So this is how helpless those kids felt when I badgered them.

Boone stumbled to a cot when his legs grew weak. *Dear God…*

There was no one there to witness his weakness now. He rolled over, wrapped his arms around himself, and sobbed until he fell asleep.

CHAPTER 9

No More Hope

The shaking of his cot stirred Boone before he was ready to wake. Three guards stood over him, ordering him to stand and follow them. Most likely he would be going to surgery for his chest and back installation. To his surprise, they headed left, away from the surgery room. The humbots took him all the way down the hall like last time but turned left to a dimly lit foyer. They opened a door and escorted Boone in.

A humbot lay on a bed on the other side of the room. When they closed the door, they locked it. Boone rushed to the door and tried to open it.

"Hello!" Boone banged on the door. "What am I suppose to do?"

The humbot moaned like a human, not a computer. That sparked Boone's curiosity enough to investigate.

When Boone got within ten feet, he recognized Sawyer's eyes and nose. The rest of him had been revamped. He raced over to him. "Sawyer, oh man, look what they've done to you..."

There was movement under his eyelids, and then they opened. It was like looking into the eyes of nothingness.

"Sawyer, it's me, Boone. Do you remember me?"

"Yes, I— believe—so. You are—correction—were my—cellmate."

"Yeah." Boone placed his hands on his arm. "You remember. That's good!"

"Where are the — others? You can — tell me."

Boone stepped away and looked suspiciously at his friend. "I have no idea where they are, Sawyer. You're the last to see them. Do you know where they are?"

Sawyer looked away and didn't say anything as if he was straining to remember. "We separated. I went — one way. They went — another."

So what Sawyer had told him after recovering from his capture was true. Sawyer didn't know where their friends were, and the humbots had brought Boone here to see if one of them would reveal where they were.

The door quickly opened, and two guards grabbed Boone. "Come, hu-man."

This time, Boone was certain he was going for surgery.

Boone opened his eyes, and even though his vision was blurred, he could tell that no one was there to soothe his worry. He moved his hand over his chest, then he gritted his teeth as he felt the indentations of foreign materials. He couldn't believe how the intensity of pain grew with each new part. They hardly allowed enough recovery time between each surgery.

Is it still my own heart? He pressed against it to see if he could feel the normal palpitations. *Yes, there it is.* It was still his own heart that made his blood flow through whatever parts remained his own.

There wasn't any reason to wake. Boone kept his eyes closed allowing sleep to pause the horrors of this nightmare.

Only a moment lapsed before the entrance door opened. *Say it isn't so; it can't be time for another surgery already.* Boone didn't move hoping they wouldn't bother him. He heard them lay another person next to his cot. A shadow hovered over him, and then he heard the robotic hum fade as they left the cell and then the chamber.

The boy moaned, so Boone rolled off of his cot to assist him. He looked younger than Boone, maybe twelve. He was a scrawny Hispanic, about five-foot-four, with a frown that was solidly embedded.

Boone was concerned about the kid's reaction when he woke because his eyebrows were furrowed. The boy reached for his left leg then began to thrash around. Boone placed his hand on the kid's chest, trying to calm him, but he became more aggressive, to the point where Boone had to step away.

The boy opened his eyes, and there was only hatred there. "Where am I, I demand to know! What have you done to me?"

"Chill out, dude. I'm in the same position you are, captured in this — this computerized nightmare."

"How do I know you're not lying to me?"

"Look around, we're both imprisoned in the same cell."

The kid swung his legs over the edge of his cot and examined his surroundings.

"My name is Boone." He extended his hand.

The boy knocked it away.

"Look, kid. You need all the friends you can get to handle what's up ahead." Boone bent over him. "Not one of us asked to be brought here. The only way we can fight this is to work as a team to get out of here."

The boy sank into the cot and crossed his arms upon his chest. Boone sat on his cot.

"So this is for real," the boy's voice was softer. "It's not a dream."

"I'm personally hoping it's the longest, most real nightmare I've had and will wake up to my normal life. I can tell you this; if I ever do get back to my real life, there's going to be a lot of changes."

There was a long pause before the boy spoke. "My name is Reed. I was pushed into my gym storage locker, and when I finally opened the door, I was here. How's that possible?"

"Do you bully kids?"

"That's none of your business!"

"I'm a bully. Every one of the kids I've met since I've been here are bullies too. We've been sent here to change our behavior permanently, by deprogramming us electronically."

"Why?"

"How much trouble did you get into? Were you suspended and only became more of a tyrant?"

Reed's jaw clenched before he spoke. "I don't like being messed with by anyone. My papa doesn't allow it, so neither do I."

"Do you pick on the computer geeks?"

"So what of it?" Reed smashed his fist into his palm.

"I did too. And so did the others. Now we're being transformed into robots to take away our hostilities toward the geeks. How's that for revenge by the nerds?"

"So you're saying all the geeks of the world have come up with this plot to get even with the bullies?"

"No." Boone stood to pace. "This is a different world. A group of my friends already escaped, and they caught one of them. They showed me where they found Sawyer, and it was so lifeless that it almost killed him. We are living in a glass bubble where this compound is maintained by life support."

Reed closed his eyes and ran his hand through his spiked black hair. He shook his head. "Why? Who would send us here to be 'deprogrammed'? I may not go to church, but I believe there's a God. Why would He allow anyone to be sent here? Are we dead, and we don't know it? Is this our hell?"

Boone's eyebrows rose as he processed Reed's questions. "I don't go to church either, but no, I don't think God has anything to do with this."

"Well, it's certainly not the evil dude, because he would celebrate our bad behavior."

"You'll drive yourself crazy if you try to figure out why we're here. We need to focus on how to get home."

The entrance door compressed, and Boone whispered, "Act like you're asleep."

They both settled in their cots and listened to the robots approach the cell. The door opened and to Boone's surprise, they went to Reed's cot. They reached for his feet and shoulders, but Reed jumped, rushing the cyborg at his feet. When the robot fell on his rump, Reed bolted from the cage. The entrance gate opened, and three humbot blocked Reed's escape. Reed stooped trying to drive through the middle robot, only to bounce off as if hitting a rock wall. He slammed into the wall behind with a thud and then slid to the floor; eyes crossed. Two guards carried Reed out.

Why did they take Reed? Boone was relieved because he only had one more phase before he was totally revamped. He paced around the edge of his cell and stopped when he saw a device under one of the cots. He knelt down and took a closer look. *So that's what a listening device looks like.*

If Boone disconnected it, he was certain that it would be replaced, so he left it alone. He looked around the walls to see if he could spot a camera. A new shelf had been installed above the entrance gate, which housed a new video camera. It was too difficult to tell if it scanned their living area. It was going to be tricky educating Reed on the details of their escape.

This was the first time since he'd been in the cell that he felt well enough to walk around. *I miss exercise!*

The entrance gate compression hissed, ending Boone's therapy. *Here we go.*

The same guards that took Reed opened the cell door. Boone willingly stood and followed them. As they led him forward, Boone watched the movement of the camera. It detected them just as they rounded the last cell. The entrance gate opened, and they led Boone to the left.

Now what's going on?

They returned Boone to the basement. Captain Babs escorted him to a different monitor.

"We have found the hu-man named Grace Gilmore."

They ran the video. Boone inhaled. It must have been the other girl who had just come in from surgery when he was on the way out.

"What have you done to her?"

The girl was bloated, and her skin looked like that of a roasted turkey.

"We did nothing. She left the safety of the compound, and thus she is now expired." The captain switched to another video. "We found Dallas with her. He will survive."

Dallas's skin looked a lot like Sawyer's did. Boone could tell that the healing agent they used on Sawyer was also restoring Dallas. "Where are the others?"

"We do not know. Do you not see that it is futile to escape?"

"Yes, I see that."

"Good. You are ready for your next surgery."

Boone took a long deep breath and stood to follow the two guards. With each procedure, more hope and courage left Boone. Maybe it was futile to escape from the compound, but there had to be a way to get home.

CHAPTER 10
"Why" Is Important

How could it be possible to hurt even more? It felt like his arms had been removed in order to attach the robotic arms. Boone moaned and moaned as he fought to wake. Even with his eyes opened it seemed so dark, so blurred. Was Reed there? He couldn't sense that anyone was there to bring comfort.

Finally Boone's eyes adjusted from the deep sleep of surgery. He looked around and found no one. Reed had to be in surgery again. Boone was grateful that they hadn't transformed him with such urgency.

The entrance gate hissed, and Boone looked to see if Reed was coming. When they opened the cell gate with someone else, he was surprised.

"Where's Reed?"

The two guards plopped the new boy in the cot next to Boone. *That was Reed's cot. What did they do with Reed?*

Boone caught a glimpse of one guard's profile and inhaled. "Sawyer, it's me, Boone. Don't you recognize me?"

Sawyer turned toward Boone. "I am SAW1958."

It was no longer Sawyer's voice, but computerized.

"Oh, Sawyer. You are totally processed."

"I am SAW1958," Sawyer repeated. "You will not detain us?"

"No." Boone felt as if every ounce of strength left him.

"We will go now." Sawyer followed the other guard out. The other guard moved forward, but Sawyer hesitated. He looked at Boone, placed his hands on two bars motioning to pull, and looked at the vent across the cell gate. Boone nodded and Sawyer did likewise, before catching up with the other guard.

A smile appeared on Boone's face as renewed hope surged in his heart. When they disappeared, Boone returned to the new inductee. How was it possible? This boy had replacements up to his waist. That took three procedures to get that far on Boone.

There was no sign of him regaining consciousness. This kid had contour to his muscles although only five feet eight inches tall. His hair was dusty brown and spiked in the front. He looked like an all-American athlete, but definitely not a bully.

The boy cried out. "Help me, oh, I hurt. My legs, my legs."

Boone took his hand and was surprised by the strength of the boy's grip. Boone squeezed back, and the boy let go. He forgot that he had more strength with the robotic arm.

The kid opened his eyes and retreated deeper into his cot.

"It's okay. I'm here to help."

"Where am I?" His voice was deeper than Boone expected.

"You're at a processing center. They're trying to stop our bully tendencies by computerizing us."

"You're kidding," he said, trying to get up. He moaned in pain. "No, you're not kidding…who are you?"

"My name's Boone, what's yours?"

"I'm Joe. So you're a bully, then why am I here?"

"You don't pick on nerds?"

"Of course not. Who sent you here?"

"Somehow my school notified this place. I ended up here. Everyone else I've met is a bully through and through. And you didn't bully anyone?"

"I just forced a computer geek to do a report for me, so I could make the baseball team. I swear I've never done anything like that before."

"Wow. If you're not a bully, you just shot down our theory."

"Well," Joe slowly added. "I may have gone a little overboard my first time out."

"What do you mean?"

"The geek is the preacher's kid. He refused to do my paper so I kept tormenting him. Doug finally did the paper, and I got a sixty percent on it. I missed the grade I needed by two percent. He did it on purpose. I didn't make the team so I rigged his gym shorts to fall off during P.E. They fell down around Doug's legs when he was jogging past the girl's softball coach. He accidently tackled Mrs. Ashurst when Doug was trying to keep his balance, and it set off a chain reaction.

"Mrs. Ashurst was in the middle of demonstrating a fast pitch, which caused the ball to go wild toward the baseball coach. Mr. Carpenter was hit in the temple, which knocked him out and made him fall into the bat rack. The bats went flying everywhere and injured several of my classmates.

"It didn't take long to figure out that it was me who sabotaged Doug's shorts. I was the only one laughing as the whole thing played out."

"That still doesn't seem as bad as what I've done."

"Well..." Joe stalled. "I couldn't let it stop there. Doug kept saying garbage, that I needed to repent, and I had enough. I lassoed a rope around his ankles and hoisted him up one of the school trees. No one found him for an hour. He was out cold, and his ankles were bruised and bleeding."

"Yep, you belong here."

"There's something else too. It's the feeling of satisfaction I got when I was tormenting Doug."

Those words hit Boone so hard he had to sit. *Yes.* Boone had never thought about what he was feeling when he was harassing one of his victims. He felt it was tough if they didn't like it because they deserved whatever he gave. It was nothing but pure self-righteous revenge on kids who outwardly had no value to him.

There was silence as they both sorted out their thoughts.

"The sad thing is," Joe eyes dampened. "I never looked down on anyone else until my parents started having marriage problems.

They split up, and on weekends when I was with my dad, it was like he's a different person. Everything I did was wrong. I felt like an idiot…like I was the one who caused the break up.

"Okay, so I lied. I am a bully. After my experience with Doug, I started mapping out other geeks to pick on."

Boone stretch out on the cot. *Wow, so that's it. I take my misery out on the weaklings who have no meaning, just because I feel like my dad thinks I'm nothing since he misses all my important events.*

"What does that make us?" Boone asked. "Bully doesn't fully define us. I'd call us monsters."

Joe sniffed, as he rolled away from Boone.

The entrance gate opened, and Boone drew a deep breath. So this was it. He would be forever lost to this manufactured world.

Sawyer was at the lead of the pack. When he entered the cell, he walked to Joe's cot. The guard behind him looked familiar. He was bulkier and a bit taller, but the same dark spiked hair poked through the helmet. It was Reed. *I can't believe his bad fortune, and now they're taking Joe.*

"Come, hu-man," Reed commanded.

"I don't want to go." Joe crossed his arms.

"Don't fight them, Joe. You don't want to go through their form of discipline."

Joe breathed in deeply and wearily stood as the pain surged through his body. "Will I see you when I get back?"

Boone tried to sound convincing. "I'll be here."

The procession of humbots coming and going sickened Boone. He sank into the cot. Then his heart leapt when he heard tapping from the vent. He raced to the cell door searching through the slats. There were the unmistakable green eyes of Taylor Twitterbum. Boone motioned for him not to say anything.

Two fingers went through the slats and curved as if grabbing something. Then Taylor slid his fingers apart. Boone nodded and went to the bars that had weak welds. He was amazed how easily the bars spread apart. It was somewhat of a tight fit, but he finally squeezed through and immediately put the bars back.

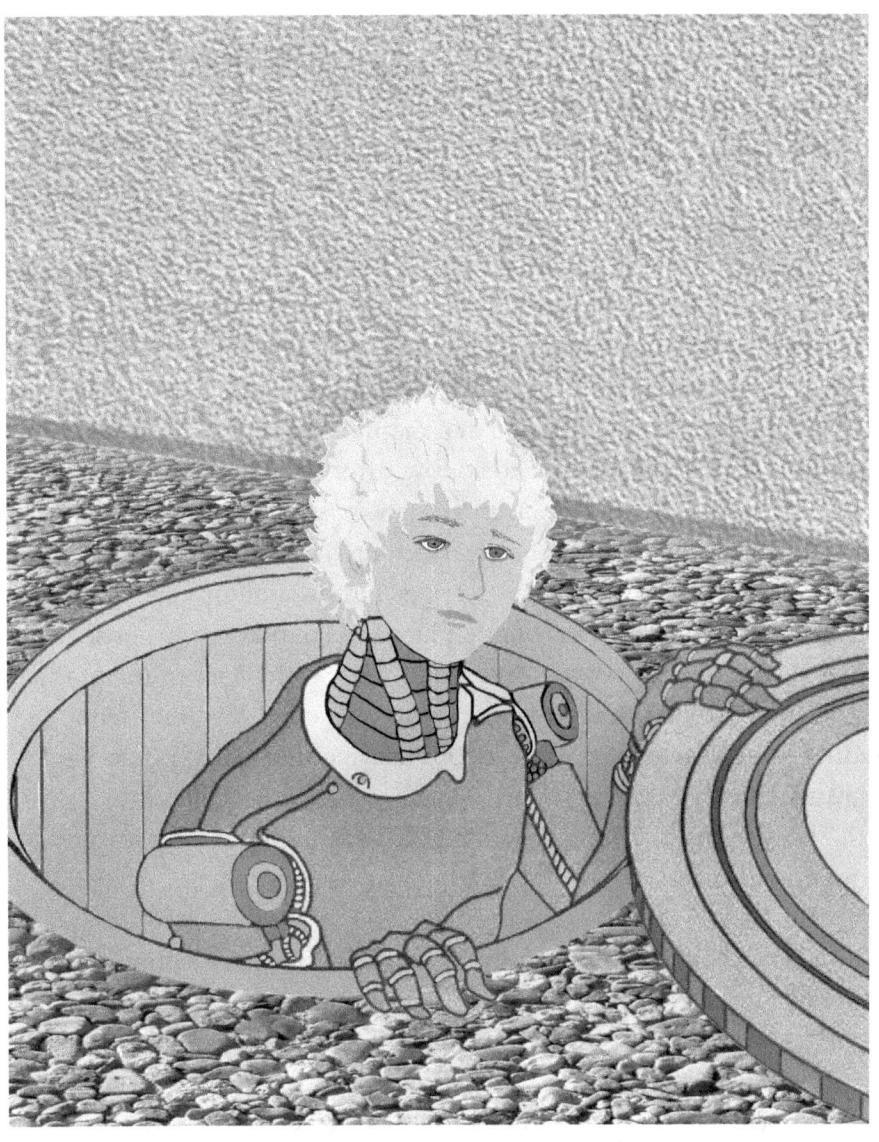

Taylor pushed the vent out after Boone's fingers grabbed hold of the grate. He slid back so that Boone could climb in and close the vent behind them. They crawled for what seemed like a mile without saying a word. Taylor knew which turn to take at every intersection. Boone gave up trying to remember.

When they came upon a vent that had no light coming through, Taylor pushed it open and slid out. Only the top of his head could be seen. The air was different but breathable, so Boone suspected they were outside the Robotic Center's compound but still within the protective bubble.

Boone attempted to speak, but Taylor put his finger to his lips. He motioned Boone onward.

There were concrete buildings everywhere and a streetlight on each corner, but it still wasn't difficult to stay in the shadows. In a dead-end alley, Taylor stopped at a manhole cover.

He motioned for Boone to follow after lifting the cover. Taylor climbed in and Boone replaced the cover with more ease than he expected after descending the steel ladder.

Twenty feet down, they stepped into a damp enclosure. It smelled of stagnant water. Boone placed his hand over his nose until Taylor handed him a cloth. There was light at the base of the ladder, signifying the manhole cover. Taylor walked a few feet from the ladder, then reached for a ledge to retrieve a flashlight. When Taylor walked several yards he finally spoke.

"They've been taking the new kids before they totally revamped you, do you know why?"

"No."

"Because they didn't totally revamp Sawyer when they did the cranial surgery. They missed connecting some vital memory avenues in his brain. He can still remember who he is."

"How do you know that?"

"Sawyer came down and talked to us. He knows where we are."

Every twelve feet, one light encased in a glass lamp helped give Boone a better look at where they were.

Drops of moisture occasionally fell from the ceiling of the tunnel, landing on top of them. Boone brushed them away until he realized it was harmless. Then out of the corner of his eyes, he saw something large move from the ledge and leap toward him. He grabbed it in midair and crushed it with his hand.

Boone quickly tossed it down when he realized it was a rat.

"You're going to come in real handy down here," Taylor said with a smile.

"What is this place? The sewer line?"

"The sewer line passes through in different areas, but as far as we can tell, its abandoned tunnels underneath the compound. We've found fresh water streams, dry tunnels, and sewage lines." Taylor dodged the puddles that were deeper.

"And the humbots don't patrol this area?"

"They haven't yet. So far it has been a great hideout. There's actually a chamber off one of these sewer veins. It's out of the raw sewage, but with waste all around, we're hoping the humbots don't think about investigating this area." Taylor continued to weave through the tunnels.

"How do you handle the smell?"

"The chamber's deep enough out of the tunnel that it doesn't smell too bad. You'll get used to it. We did."

"How come Sawyer wandered out of the compound barrier when you guys escaped?"

"We were all trying to find a way home. You said something about going for a haircut and ended up here. How?"

"I asked my barber how high the chair went, and the chair rose clear through the ceiling. An elevator door opened into a robotic school of some sort. A robot by the name of…"

"Regu?" Taylor helped.

"Yes! That's the dude. Did you meet him too?"

"He must be like the Walmart greeter. Welcome to Robot world, may I have your brain?" Taylor moved robotically.

"Dude. That isn't even funny."

"Sorry, my bad."

Boone's eyebrows arched. "How did you get here?"

"I was at the mall with a friend. He challenged me to go up the down-flowing escalator in two minutes. When I reached the top, I ended up in the same small elevator."

They walked in silence for several minutes. The tunnel looked like it had been carved out much like a ground squirrel would carve his tunnels; only honed stone encased the areas where the dirt pathway had to be reinforced.

Crevices appeared sporadically in the side of the tunnel where rock walls were formed through years of expanding and contracting with the movement of the Earth. A two-foot gap appeared to their right, and Taylor stopped. "Watch your head."

The tunnel widened quickly and took many turns before a door appeared. Taylor opened it, and Boone was surprised by what he saw.

CHAPTER 11
Nowhere To Go

The girl named Joy, who had escaped with Taylor, was sitting in a circle with several teens in various stages of revamping. Boone's eyes widened when he saw Sawyer and bolted for the door.

"It's okay, Boone," Taylor reassured him.

Sawyer approached Boone to shake his hand and said in his real voice, "I'm sorry I had to deceive you, Boone."

"You're all right!" Boone returned his handshake with more enthusiasm. "They didn't revamp you?"

"Well, yes and no. They have equipped me with all the components because it's easy to switch on the computerized voice, but somehow they messed up on connecting the memory and brain functions."

"Sawyer's the reason why they haven't totally processed you."

"I feel bad about revamping Reed so quickly, and now Joe. Every time they placed you on the docket, I put someone else down. It was getting close when no new bullies were coming in. That's why we had to get you out once your robotic arms were working."

"The manhunt's really going to pick up now that you're gone, Boone," Taylor said.

"Speaking of, I better get back to it, or they'll start adding things up. I'm working from the inside to figure out how to get us home."

"Good! Then there *is* hope."

"Always."

Taylor led Boone to the group. "Let's introduce you to some of these kids. Joy you already know. Let's go over here."

There were eight of them, including Sawyer. Boone's head was spinning, trying to remember their names and where they came from.

Taylor took Boone to a makeshift couch made out of items found at the compound's trash site. As each child was robotized, the humbots discarded their clothes, which provided ample supplies to make beds, pillows, and blankets. When Boone sank into the couch, it was the most comfort he had felt since he entered the cells. He relaxed and quickly fell asleep.

Boone sniffed at the delicious aroma and his eyes quickly opened.

Aw man! He slammed his fist into the bedding when he realized he wasn't home. But the food sitting on the end table did look enticing. He quickly reached for the bottled water and drained it. He couldn't imagine where they found the supplies, but he didn't care. Boone devoured the meat on the plate and didn't slow down on the carrots and mashed potatoes. What a welcomed meal after being served watery soup in the cell.

Taylor entered the chambers. "How did you like the roasted rat?"

Boone spit out the carrot he just placed in his mouth. It was too late to expel the meat.

"Just kidding."

"Oh man." Boone's jaw clenched as he tried to remain seated and not pounce on Taylor. "You're worse than my older brother. So what is it really? I've never tasted anything like it."

"It's quail. There seems to be a lot of them within the compound."

"Where did you get these carrots and potatoes?"

"You don't want to know."

"No, really."

"Did you sleep well?" Taylor changed the subject.

"Yes, I did. But I have a few questions. Why did Grace go outside the compound with Sawyer?"

"We didn't know she followed Sawyer. She kept asking if she could go with him and we said no, but she slipped out without us knowing it."

"So has Sawyer come up with anything on how to get out of here?"

"Not yet."

"Where are the others?" Boone asked.

"That's where the vegetables come from. We all go out and scavenge for food when someone's resting here. But right now we need your help."

"Okay, I'm all in."

"We've decided to rescue all new kids coming into the compound. Joe hasn't been totally revamped yet. They just installed his chest and back gear and dropped him off in the cell. We want you to go and bring him here. You're the only one who has robotic strength in your arms besides Sawyer."

"Absolutely, just give me a layout of all the turns I need to make in the ventilation ducts."

Taylor pulled a small map out of his pocket. "I'll take you as far as the entry point of the duct."

"I'm ready. Lead the way."

He was surprised how the dank smell didn't overpower him like before.

As Taylor led the way, Boone grew more confused. "I hope I can find my way back here."

"I've taken all forks to the right. When you come back, take all lefts." Taylor stopped. "This is where we go up. If I'm alone, I put this flashlight back in the crevice just a few feet from the ladder."

When both of them reached the top, Boone wondered if he had slept a whole day because it was still dark.

A cadence of humbots passed the alley. Taylor rushed to lower the manhole cover, then grasped Boone's arm to drag him into a shadow.

One humbot stopped at the alley entrance and turned toward them. Taylor and Boone flopped to the ground when a light shined on the opposite side of the alley. The guard swept the light just above them, and then disappeared.

Taylor motioned Boone to follow. When they got to the end of the building, Taylor gestured to the compound unit just down the street, handed Boone a small flashlight and gave him a thumbs up.

It was much different without Taylor as his guide. With every movement or sound, Boone crouched to the ground. Boone didn't remember seeing this many humbots roaming the streets when Taylor helped him escape.

Boone removed the cover off of the duct and froze when he heard the rhythm of footsteps. He quickly slid in and held the ventilation cover in place with his fingers curled around the grate.

Peering between the slats, a trickle of sweat rolled into Boone's left eye. The line of humbots seemed endless... *Come on, come on.* His fingers started to cramp, sending spasms up his arm. The cover rattled so he moved it away from wall. The last guard paused. *Oh man!*

"Come REE1935," Boone heard a humbot call out. *That's got to be Reed.*

The young humbot returned to the group and moved on.

Boone exhaled and waited another minute. He lifted the cover to hook it on to the clips, and leaned back against the duct wall. Even though his pulse was racing, for the moment he felt safe. How he wished that feeling would remain. The constant feeling of doom clung to him like a ball and chain attached to his leg.

This whole experience mirrored the cruelties he thrust upon Dexter and his nerdy friends. *Isn't this lesson a bit more sadistic then anything I've done?*

No. He lowered his head in shame. *Those kids felt the same fear and dread I'm going through now.*

As Boone approached an intersection, he heard voices from the opposite direction of where he was supposed to go. He wanted to listen in, but that was something he would do another time. The temptation to investigate slowed Boone down when the smell of food, or music came from vents he passed. It was taking a lot longer than when Taylor led the way.

After Boone came to the end of the line, he peered out of the vent and saw Joe lying on his cot. There was no sound, so Boone pushed open the cover and laid it against the wall.

Joe's head popped up with a look of relief. Boone put his finger to his lips as Joe rushed to the gate then followed him to the weakened bars. When Boone stretched them wider this time, one bar separated from the weld. Boone rolled his eyes and motioned Joe to come out. Boone frowned at the break in the bar after straightening it. There was nothing he could do about it now.

Boone entered the air duct with Joe close behind. Once the vent cover was latched, they made a quick trek outside the compound. Boone kept motioning for Joe to keep quiet.

They didn't come across any more patrols and made it quickly to the manhole cover. It was rare to have a moment of peace. Joe wanted to linger on the steel steps, but Boone pressed on.

Boone handed Joe a rag. "This will help you get used to the smell." Boone retrieved the flashlight in the crevice and handed it to Joe. They started down the line until Boone abruptly stopped. Computerized voices echoed through the tunnel. He hoped that wasn't near their hideout, but it was definitely coming from that direction.

Boone clasped Joe's arm and spun him the other way. They dodged the puddles as they rushed further into the tunnel. Boone wildly shined his flashlight from each side trying to find a hiding place.

The voices became louder as they neared the intersection going to the sewer line. Boone counted six distinct voices and could see lights flashing in the tunnel as they approached. They flicked their flashlights off and leaned against one side of the wall, moving slowly by braille.

A divot opened in the wall so Boone shoved Joe in then followed. They watched as Reed and two other guards marched Taylor, Joy, and four other kids toward the manhole ladder.

A two-inch washer that attached one guard's knee to his leg popped off and rolled down the tunnel right in front of where Boone and Joe hid. Boone squished Joe against the wall. Joe rested his trembling hands against Boone's back. It felt like Boone's heart was going to beat out of his chest.

The guard swept his light and finally found the washer. Boone closed his eyes and held his ragged breath as the guard lowered to retrieve the washer. The humbot grasped it and went back to the ladder. Boone gave Joe more room and felt him starting to slump, so he moved against him again.

The uneven clanging against the ladder sounded like the guard could no longer bend that knee. It took him forever to reach the top.

When all was quiet, Boone turned around to ease Joe's fall to the ground, and then stepped out of the divot to check things out. There was no sign of lights shining on the wall or sounds coming from the area of the hideout.

Joe coughed and tried to stand. Boone helped him to his feet. "Wow, dude, give a guy some room to breathe."

"Sorry, Joe. We need to keep moving in case they come back."

"Give me a second." Joe leaned over. "How close did they come?"

"If that humbot had just looked to his right, we'd be heading to the cells with the rest of them."

"Okay, I'm ready to go."

Boone turned on the flashlight and started in the opposite direction of the hideout. "Look for a sizable crevice in the wall that might go deeper. It's not safe to go back to the hideout."

They heard clanking over every manhole cover they passed. When they came to a section that had bars preventing any further travel in that vein of the tunnel, Boone said, "That must be the end of the protective bubble."

Joe tapped Boone on the shoulder and pointed his flashlight at a sizeable crack in the wall. Boone lowered himself through it and found another hallway just like the one leading to the hiding place. A door with a padlock on it was at the end of the hall. Boone placed it in his hand and easily crumbled it.

When they shined their lights inside, there were boxes stacked on top of each other. The outside of the boxes read: manna-fruit, manna-vegetables, manna-meats, manna-milk, and manna-juices.

"Here's a box marked lanterns." Joe quickly opened it and found everything needed to light it. They each took a lantern and checked for listening devices. When they were certain there were none, they closed the door and felt safe to speak for the first time.

"Where have I heard that word before?" Boone asked.

"Manna? It's what God fed the Israelites in the wilderness, with that Moses dude."

"Oh yeah. Were you forced to go to church?"

"Nope, Sunday school when I was a wee boy."

"That's an interesting choice of word to put on those boxes," Boone said. "Let's see what else is here."

"Why do you think this food is here?" Joe eagerly checked out boxes.

"I have no clue. By the cobwebs, it looks like no one's been here for years. Let's find something to eat, and then we can plan what to do."

Boone found tuna fish, pears, asparagus, and apple juice. Joe chose chicken, peaches, corn, and cranberry juice. Boone couldn't believe their good fortune then grimaced when he thought about his friend's bad fortune.

"It's nice to have a little bit of heaven in this nightmare." Boone belched with satisfaction.

"So what do you think they'll do to the others?"

"They step up the processing when any of us cause trouble. I wonder if they realize Sawyer hasn't been totally revamped."

"Who's that?"

"He's the first one here before Taylor then I came. He escaped, left the protective bubble of the Robotics Center and almost died.

"They did the last phase of revamping on him, but somehow messed up on the connections, so Sawyer's been acting as a double agent. He's trying to find where we entered this place so we can leave." Boone put away his garbage.

"Did you notice that other kid that came before me? He's total humbot now."

"It's eerie to watch someone you've been talking to go through the changes. It's hard to believe they are so completely against you after trying to help find a way out of here."

"So what are we going to—" Joe stopped when they heard someone outside the door. They both grabbed their lanterns and blew them out.

The door squealed as it opened. The silhouette of Sawyer framed the doorway. Something wasn't right though. He now had a light in the middle of his forehead. It was flashing red.

CHAPTER 12
Home Away From Home

Boone grabbed Joe and dashed to the left of the boxes to hide in the back. The cases of food provided narrow passage where they could dodge one guard, but if Sawyer came with more than one humbot, it would be just a matter of time before they were caught.

"Did you see that?" a guard asked.

"No," Sawyer said.

"It is obvious they are in here. There are heat waves coming from those lanterns. I will go to the right of the boxes. You check the left."

Joe tried to move to the middle, but Boone stopped him, hoping that Sawyer hadn't been discovered as a traitor. Their only chance was to stay in the left row and test Sawyer's loyalty. They would be caught anyway, even if Sawyer had become a full cyborg.

Boone placed his hand over Joe's mouth, as Joe strained to hide elsewhere. Sawyer locked eyes with Boone and hesitated. A bead of sweat rolled down Joe's face as he looked from Boone to Sawyer. Boone lifted Joe to move farther in the row allowing Sawyer passage. Sawyer went all the way to the back, and Boone followed so that the other guard coming down the right side wouldn't see them through the adjacent aisle. Boone released Joe and placed his finger to his lips.

"You did not find them?" the guard asked when they met in the middle back row.

"They must have left the room just before we arrived."

"Let us go down the middle. If we do not find them, we will look elsewhere."

Time crawled as they examined the middle row.

"Let us take these." The guard clanged the lanterns together.

When they finally left, they heard the guards put a new padlock on the outside of the door. It was now pitch black. Boone reached into his pocket and flicked on his flashlight. Joe moved to the door and tried to open it, but it wouldn't budge. Boone rummaged through the box of lanterns and produced two more.

"This is my last match. I hope we find more." Boone flashed it against his plated body and lit the lanterns. They leaned against the first row of boxes and sighed.

"Well, if we have to be prisoners, I'd rather be here," Joe said.

"Let's get some rest, and then figure out what to do."

Joe immediately fell to sleep, but Boone kept running rescue plans through his mind. It appeared that the humbots were aware of every crevice in the tunnels. What chance did they have to find a safe haven? The only way they would be able to find a way home was to be outside the cells. If they could get out of this food chamber, then they needed to find another hideout. Somehow the safe haven they originally were in had been discovered by the cyborgs.

Joe rolled over trying to find a comfortable spot. He raised his left arm behind his head then settled. A needle-sized laser flashed into Boone's eyes before hitting the wall across the room. It originated from under Joe's arm.

Boone crawled next to Joe and found some kind of radar device that the surgeons implanted where the armpit would be attached on the next surgery. Boone raised his left arm and searched for the same thing.

"Joe, wake up." Boone tapped his leg.

"Huh, what?"

"Do you see this?" Boone pointed at his device.

Joe rubbed the sleep out of his eyes and then looked. "What is that?"

"That, my friend, is how they have been finding us. I have a feeling they know Sawyer is helping us, and they know we're here. Let's see if we can take these off."

Boone leaned in closely to examine Joe's device. "I think it'll pop out of the pocket if we can find something to pry it out."

"How about that utensil box?" Joe dug through the box and returned with a fork. Boone broke off the two outside prongs and used the middle to pick the device. It easily popped off when Boone found the correct angle.

"Let me check the other side. I think you're all clear." Boone lifted his arm. "My turn."

They laid the devices on top of a box.

"Can I smash them?"

"I think we should lay them apart but in the same area, and keep them here. When we find a way out of here tomorrow and find another hiding place, we can just leave these here. That way they won't know we've found them right away, and maybe we can move some of these boxes of food."

"I like how you think," Joe said. "Did you get any rest?"

"No. Maybe we better take shifts. You go first."

"Fine by me." Joe snuggled into his blanket and closed his eyes.

As hard as Boone tried, he couldn't shut down his mind. How would he rescue his friends before they were revamped? Would they ever get the chance to find their way home, or would they forever be on the run from the humbot patrol? Fatigue finally won and Boone drifted to sleep.

———

"Boone." Joe shook him. "Boone, wake up."

Boone jerked and took a swing at Joe.

"It's me, Joe. Be quiet, I think they're back."

They grabbed their lanterns and rushed to the furthest row of boxes. Only one of the lanterns were dimly lit, and Joe blew it out just before the door swung open. A steady low-pitched beeping grew more rapid as they approached the boxes.

"They found the radar devices."

"I told you they were not here," Sawyer stated. "If you had not forgotten our detectors, we would not have had to return."

"Now it will be impossible for us to find them. Our only hope is if they try to contact you; you can lead us to them."

"That has always been the plan. We might as well return to headquarters."

They shuffled out of the chamber and closed the door.

Joe and Boone waited several minutes before they moved.

"I don't think they locked the door." Boone cautiously ventured out of hiding. He slowly opened the door and stopped when it started to squeal. "Let's wait a little bit longer. Is there any oil in those boxes?"

"I think so. I'll check."

With the door oiled, they went to the main stream of the tunnels. Joe automatically turned to the left, but Boone stood looking through the bars that ended their passage.

"What are you looking at?"

"Come here." Boone pointed through the bars. "Can you see that shadow to the right about ten feet down?"

"Yeah. What do you think it is?"

"I wonder if that's an access point to another cove. It would be the perfect hiding spot because the guards wouldn't think of looking past the bars."

"Nice thought, but how will we get past the bars?" Joe tried to shake one. "It's probably outside the safety barrier of the compound."

Boone handed Joe his lantern. He wrapped his fingers around one bar and tried to spin it. When it turned, Boone lifted the bar up and down as he rotated it. The bar eventually had enough room to lift out from the bottom. Boone laid the bar against the wall and squeezed through the sixteen-inch opening. Joe went through with ease.

The shadow was an indentation in the wall that led to a hallway farther away from the tunnel. The path narrowed and inclined, then stopped.

"Well, it was a great idea."

"Wait a minute, Joe." Boone reached for Joe's lantern. "I feel air coming from the corner of this wall."

They looked closely and found two handholds. Joe tugged on the wall and it glided with ease. The entrance was a small six-by-ten feet room and then widened out to a large chamber. The room was outfitted with a large table, meeting room chairs, an area that could be used for food preparation, and a living room area with chairs. Another hall led to rooms with bunk beds.

"Is this for real?" Joe danced around as he touched everything.

"I guess the bars are to keep runaways from making a home here. Let's start moving some of the food over here. We now have a basis for a plan."

Boone and Joe went back to the storage room and found several backpacks. They opened boxes in the last three rows of food and transferred them into packs so that the empty boxes would remain in the storage room, as if they were still full.

There was a reminiscent feeling of home as Joe and Boone stored different food items in the cabinets.

"I miss home." Joe stacked cans of fruit in a cupboard. "I didn't think I would ever feel that way."

"Why do you say that?"

"I'm an only child. Part of the reason my parents divorced is my dad was always gone on maneuvers in the military. He ended up being killed in Iraq. My mother worked hard to keep a roof over our heads and food on the table. Then she married a man who was abusive. When I tried to defend her, he took after me.

"I never thought I'd turn on others who are weaker then me and harass them, because of what my stepfather does to me, but something snapped inside of me." Joe stopped unpacking and sat.

"Talk about being in denial. You swore you weren't a bully."

"I guess I see my weakness in my victims as I badger them. They're pathetic, and that mirrors how I see myself. Since I came to this robotic nightmare, I see how I've allowed my worry and misery decide how I look at life. I need to find solutions instead of being part of the problem."

"What would you do differently if you were home?"

"I'd talk to my mother and tell her that I'm concerned for her safety. If she won't do anything, I'll go to a counselor at school and see if I can get help through an adult."

"And if that doesn't work, then what?"

"I'll go to the police department and file a complaint and call immediately after he beats my mom or me. When I say I miss home, I mean what it was like before my mom hooked up with John."

"I'm sorry you have to go through that, Joe." Boone grew quiet as he thought about what he had to face when he got home. He was certain that some time in detention would be part of it. "Let's get some rest. I need to find out what's happening with Taylor and Dallas tomorrow."

CHAPTER 13
The Wrestling Match

———

Boone left Joe behind in the safety of their cubby. As he approached the cells through the ventilation system, he hoped that Taylor and Dallas were still there, or it would mean that they had been completely revamped.

The rhythm of robots marching past the cellblock vent halted Boone's movement. Three of them carried Dallas out of the cell. Sawyer was the last to shut the door, and Boone frowned when he saw the changes that had been made. There were no longer bars on the cell. Metal walls went all the way up, leaving only a small window on the cell door, which was impossible to crawl through even with the bars torn out.

When all was silent, Boone removed the vent cover and walked over to the door. Taylor's back was to him, so he tapped on it. Taylor moved quickly to the door, which moved when he leaned against it. They both smiled, realizing that Sawyer was still a team player.

Boone made sure that no one else was in the cells, and then retreated. Taylor had already entered the ventilation duct and was deep within. It wasn't until outside the holding compound, that Boone was able to catch him.

Boone motioned for Taylor to lift his arms and pointed at the radar. It only took a second to pop it off, sending it to the ground. Taylor didn't hesitate to smash it underfoot.

As they scurried from shadow to shadow, the sound of guards behind them quicken their pace. It was amazing they didn't intercept them right outside the holding compound. They feared they wouldn't be able to use the ducts to gain access to the cells any longer.

Once they made it to the tunnels, Boone retrieved the hidden flashlight and moved Taylor rapidly to the right. Each manhole entrance they passed had humbots lifting covers off and clambering down the ladders.

The army was making such a racket; Taylor and Boone didn't try to hide the noise of their frenzied escape. When the bars at the end of the line appeared in front of them, Taylor panicked.

"Now where are we going to go? Can't you hear them? They're right behind us."

Boone slid the loose bar up and out and motioned Taylor forward. Boone squeezed through and replaced the bar. They entered the hallway and doused the flashlight just as lights appeared around the bend of the tunnel. Boone and Taylor huddled together, trying to steady their breathing. They didn't dare move.

The troop immediately went to the storage facility. Boone grabbed Taylor and scrambled up the darkened corridor to the hidden door of their new home.

The movement of the door startled Joe. "You found—" Boone made a motion for silence. In a matter of seconds they heard noise from the direction of the storage room, which was on the other side of the wall in the cubby. The search didn't last long. All eyes were wide as they heard the procession of cyborgs leave the storage area.

It became too quiet, too fast. None of the teens moved. Then they leapt as they grabbed for each other when the spasmodic clanging of pans raked across the bars. They turned in unison expecting their enemies to knock out the loose bar and find their hiding place.

Their breathing quickened as they focused on the entrance. And they waited...and waited.

After several minutes in silence, they all moved to a chair, but continued to hold vigilance over the entrance. Boone couldn't handle the suspense any longer. He slowly slid the door open and moved into the entrance hall. Rays from a multitude of flashlights shining through the bars, finally quit. Boone stepped back into the cubby and slid the door shut.

They moved to the table and sat staring at each other. No one was willing to speak until they were certain they would not be heard.

"We've got to be careful from this time forward," Boone whispered. "Even though there's an appearance of safety here, we must realize that we can be heard if they're in the storage room, or even standing by the bars."

Taylor leaned forward. "I wish we could set up a system to notify us when they are approaching the bars.

"We'll have to think about that one," Joe said.

Boone got up and prepared some food. Taylor's eyes enlarged when Boone produced a meal with meat, vegetable, and fruit.

"Where'd you get all this?"

"That rustling you heard through the wall is a storeroom of food. Or I at least I hope they left the food. Where did you get the food you gave me at the other hideout?"

Taylor bit into potato. "Sawyer was supplying some of it. I wonder how long we can count on Sawyer giving us an edge over the humbots. Don't you think they've figured out that Sawyer's not totally converted?"

"I imagine once they catch us all and know we can't escape anymore, that will be Sawyer's last day of freedom. So what happened to Joy?"

"They took her in for her last surgery just before they took Dallas. Dallas is being totally revamped now. If it wasn't for Sawyer, we would both be humbots."

"I saw that they didn't put metal walls between each cell."

"So far they are just putting them around the outside. You're the lucky one so far, Joe. They've only gone to your hips."

"I don't think any of us are lucky, since we're all being singled out. How are we going to help the new ones coming in?"

"We need to focus on how to get home," Boone suggested. "If we keep rescuing kids as they come in, we'll never find a way out of this nightmare."

"Do you think Sawyer has found anything out yet?" Joe finished his last bite.

"The only way we'll be able to find that out is if one of us stays in the storage room. Sawyer is the only one who has seen us there. Maybe he'll try to meet us alone."

"Yeah, but you're taking a big risk," Taylor said. "He's still wearing a homing device."

"It's a chance we're going to have to take."

"If any of us are captured, it will mean the end of all of us." Joe cleaned off his plate. "They'll find a way to track us down."

"Sometimes I think we're fighting a losing battle." Taylor lowered his head.

"We can't give up."

"You're right, Joe." Boone drained the last of his water. "I think after we eat and rest, things will look brighter."

Taylor and Joe were sleeping, so Boone ventured to the storage room. He couldn't believe the destruction that the humbots had done. The first row of boxes were opened and scattered about the room. Boone filled packs and moved the empty boxes to the back.

Two hours passed, so Boone took a break and grabbed a bottle of apple juice that was on the floor.

While sitting on top of a box in the middle of the room, the door slowly opened. Boone jumped to his feet and wondered why Sawyer lingered in the doorway. Sawyer looked behind, and then closed the door.

"I'm glad to see you, Boone. They're really having trouble finding your new hideout. That's good."

Boone looked into Sawyer's brown eyes to determine whether he could trust him. It was becoming more and more difficult to believe he had not been totally revamped. "Yeah, I came here hoping I could talk to you, Sawyer."

"I don't know how much longer they'll allow my personality memory banks to be active."

"I'm glad they have, or we would have been captured long ago. Have you found a way to get home yet?"

"They're keeping me so busy that I haven't had time to search. Plus they keep a close watch on me. I had to ditch Dallas in order to be here now."

The door slammed open, and Dallas shouted, "The Directive was correct! You are aiding the hu-mans!"

Sawyer didn't delay to rush Dallas, slamming both fists into his chest. Dallas flew backward and rolled into a somersault, landing on his feet. The blue light in the middle of Dallas's helmet flashed before a ray of light flared. Sawyer dodged the flash, which made a divot in the rock floor the size of a fist.

With three large steps, Sawyer flew into the air feet first. His robotic boots landed squarely on Dallas's abdomen, sending him against the wall, then onto the floor. Dallas was only stunned for a moment, but Sawyer didn't lose the momentum of his attack. He knelt down on top of Dallas's legs with his right leg and thrust his left arm against Dallas's throat.

Dallas wrenched Sawyer's arm away and flung him aside like a rag doll. The strength he showed caught Sawyer by surprise. Dallas stood, and the light on his helmet flickered before flashing. Sawyer rolled out of the way and swept his legs against Dallas's ankles, knocking him to the ground. Sawyer sprang on top of Dallas and went for his throat with both hands. Sawyer knelt on top of Dallas's upper arms and pinned him.

Dallas tried to rock his legs over the top of Sawyer's head, but Sawyer leaned forward, out of his reach.

Boone watched the color of Dallas's face go from beet red to white.

"Sawyer, you're killing him!"

The look on Sawyer's face was total hatred.

Boone pulled at Sawyer's shoulders. "Sawyer, stop it, you don't want to kill him!"

Sawyer let loose with one hand and shoved Boone to the ground. Boone scrambled to his feet and dove on top of Sawyer. That released Sawyer's hold on Dallas and sent Boone and Sawyer into a tangled mess. Sawyer easily brushed Boone aside and returned to Dallas. He bent down and crashed his right fist across Dallas's temple, causing his helmet to separate from his head. That finally stopped Sawyer's rampage. He backed away, and Boone rushed to Dallas, kneeling beside him. Boone placed his finger on his throat and felt a pulse.

"He's alive."

Sawyer retrieved the helmet, tentacles dangling from inside. Boone and Sawyer found ports throughout Dallas's skull where the tentacles attached. They wondered why there was no bleeding, only red dots where the connection had been terminated.

"Were you trying to kill him?" Boone furrowed his brows.

"No, I..." Sawyer raised his hands to the back of his head. "I was just ticked off. I couldn't stop the rage."

"Well, we've got to do something with him." Boone raised Dallas's left arm. Boone slid his extraction tool under the detector and popped it off.

"So that's where the homing devices are located."

Boone handed it to Sawyer. Sawyer crushed it, and then raised his own left arm.

"Unless you plan on ramping up my complete robotization by disappearing, I wouldn't remove that. They'll send an all-out hunt if you disappear with Dallas. You'll do us more good on the inside."

"I am watching kids turned into robots and it's driving me mad! Do you really think they don't know about me and that I have a chance to find a way out of here?"

"Right now you're our only hope."

Dallas moved, blinking his eyes, then asked in his human voice, "Where are we?" Just as quickly as his eyes opened, they closed.

Boone felt for his pulse. "He's okay."

"Do you think these helmets are the control center for our robotics?"

"That would be my guess." Boone handed Sawyer the helmet.

"So what are we going to do?"

"I'm going to get Taylor and Joe to help me move Dallas to our new hide-out, and you're going to take Dallas's helmet and ditch it in the opposite direction of these tunnels. Then you're going to make up a convincing story of what happened to Dallas."

"Okay, I'll come up with a story about Dallas."

Boone escorted Sawyer back to the tunnel. "You're doing good, Sawyer. Just try to control that rage. That's what gave me a one way ticket to this robot farm."

"Right." Sawyer jostled the helmet in his hands. "I'll see you soon."

Boone watched Sawyer go around the bend and listened for the splashing of the water through the tunnel to stop before he moved toward the bars. Taylor and Joe were already removing the loose bar.

"Come on, guys, I need your help."

"What the heck was going on?" Taylor asked. "It sounded like a wrestling match from the other side of the wall."

"Dallas followed Sawyer to the storage room. Sawyer disconnected the helmet from Dallas with one blow and it knocked him out, but he came to long enough to find out he's not under control of the humbots anymore. We need to move him to the cubby."

"Is that wise?" Joe asked.

"Sawyer destroyed his homing device. Unfortunately they'll know that his transmission stopped here. They'll really do a thorough search now."

Boone explained in detail what happened as they lifted Dallas and transported him to their new quarters. They placed him in the first bunkroom, and Joe volunteered to stay with him as Boone and Taylor prepared food.

Joe raced into the kitchen. "He's waking up."

"I'll stay with the food," Taylor said.

Dallas was trying to get out of bed when they returned to the bunkroom, but stopped when he saw Boone.

"Where am I? How did I get here?"

"You're safe now, Dallas." Boone placed his hand on his shoulder. "Just rest easy."

"The last thing I remember is being taken to surgery."

"We're underground, in a living quarter we found at the end of the tunnels under the robotics compound. No one has found us yet. You followed Sawyer to see if he would lead you to us."

"I was going to turn you in?"

"You would have if Sawyer hadn't knocked off your helmet and disconnected the relay to their information center."

Dallas touched the top of his head. "It is sore there."

Taylor entered the room with food and placed a tray in the middle of them. Dallas inhaled the food and asked for more. The boys filled Dallas in on everything that had happened up to the point of his surgery, and then left Dallas to rest as they wandered to a quiet place to settle in for the night.

CHAPTER 14
Total Control

———∾∾———

Dallas was still sleeping when the others woke. They placed items on the kitchen counter and prepared to move more food from the storage area to their cubby. Just as they were leaving, Dallas came out of the bunkroom.

"Hey. Are you going to leave me behind?"

"Oh, good morning, Dal." Joe put two packs over his shoulders.

"Why don't you get a start on the supplies guys, and I'll prepare something for Dallas." Boone put down his packs and returned to the kitchen.

"Sounds good." Taylor led the way. "We'll see you over there."

Boone fixed some oatmeal with raisins, brown sugar, and cinnamon and then made a batch of scrambled eggs from an egg mix. It wasn't quite home cooking, but Dallas was thrilled.

"So what's the plan?" Dallas handed Boone his empty plate.

"We're going to move as much food as we can today. We don't know how long it'll be until they start removing it. They seem to be checking it daily now."

"Okay. Count me in."

"Why don't you rest another day, and then we'll put you to work."

"What are you, my mother? I'm going to do my part to get us home."

Joe returned with his first load and quickly unpacked.

"I didn't mean to baby you, Dal. Let me show you where this goes, and then you can go with me on the next run."

"That sounds better."

As Joe left for his second run, Taylor came in with his first load.

Boone lifted his packs to his shoulder after Dallas started loading the supplies into the cabinets. When Boone slid the cave wall back to enter the tunnel hallway, he heard several splashes in the canal down the line. Glancing around the canal wall, Boone watched Sawyer lead a pack of five other humbots into the storage room. Boone was grateful that Joe had replaced the bar in the slot.

Helplessness and cowardice overshadowed Boone as he listened to Joe take on the six cyborgs. Boone watched Joe stumble into the slurry of the tunnel with his hands and feet shackled.

"You guys are computer trash who are nothing but an organized geek squad," Joe spewed. "Sure, you're eliminating the bullies from Earth, but look at what you're becoming. You're far worse then all of the bullies put together."

"Shut down, hu-man," the cyborg said.

"You can't even say 'shut up' the right way."

The other four humbots had their arms loaded with boxes of food. It wouldn't take long for them to empty the storeroom. When they rounded the corner and Boone couldn't hear splashing through the tunnel, he decided to try and retrieve at least one load before they returned.

As Boone entered the storage room, he wondered if Joe would break under pressure if they tortured him. He couldn't worry about that now. The box where the packs were stored was easy to find. Boone loaded four packs and slid two to each shoulder.

When he approached the tunnel, he paused to listen. All was quiet, so Boone dropped two packs by the bars, squeezed through, and took the other two to the entrance of the cubby. While retrieving the others, Boone could hear splattering from a distance and quickly passed through the bars only to fumble as he replaced the bar. It fell into an area with mud at the bottom.

Boone raced to the cubby entrance, laid the packs there, and rushed to the bars. Slipping his hand into the muck, Boone wrapped his fingers around the bar. It was slick, which made Boone almost drop it several times. He finally slid it back into place, and then ran his fingers over the bar, hoping to make it look as dry as the others.

The patrol was rounding the corner when Boone stepped into the passage. From the sound of it, there was more this time. Boone could see the bar from where he stood. There was a glob of mud flowing down the top of the bar. He held his breath, praying that it didn't drop.

Boone watched as the last humbot entered the hall to the storage room. The blob fell from the bar and splashed into the puddle. The humbot stepped out of the hallway and approached the bars, examining beyond them. Boone leaned against the wall, trying to breathe because he felt faint.

Finally the guard stepped away and continued to the storage room. Boone gathered the four packs and placed them at the feet of the cubby door.

When he opened the door, Dallas and Taylor were standing on each side with a chair in hand.

"It's me."

"Where's…?"

"They got Joe," Boone murmured.

They lifted the other two packs and took them to the kitchen table. Sinking into chairs, they listened to the humbots rummage through the storage room.

Boone found a pad of paper and pencil and wrote, "It's going to be a long day of not talking."

Dallas nodded as he grabbed the paper and pencil. "Do you think they will make Joe tell where we are?"

"Time's going to tell on that one." Boone wrote. "I'm glad Sawyer doesn't know where we are."

Taylor wrote. "Was he with them again?"

"He was leading five of them when they got Joe. I'm not sure if he was with this group now."

It grew quiet from the other side of the cave wall, but they still didn't say anything. It was a wise decision because within ten minutes, more noise came from the storage room.

"They must be sending in the whole troop to wipe out the resources." Boone wrote. He pointed to the overstuffed chairs, and they made themselves comfortable. Dallas and Taylor nodded off to sleep, and Boone had to fight not doing so as well. He wanted to make sure they didn't snore.

Within an hour it grew silent, and Boone kept watch for another hour.

It was the sound of Dallas snoring that woke him. He lurched to shake Dallas. Dallas's eyes opened wide.

"Sorry," he mouthed.

Boone looked at the clock on the counter and saw that two hours had passed. He went to the kitchen and quietly prepared a meal. In another hour, Boone decided to check what was going on. Dallas insisted on going with him. Taylor stayed behind.

There wasn't a sound as they approached the canal. Boone ventured to the bars. It was the first time Dallas had been out since they carried him to the cubby.

Boone shook his head when they got to the storage room. "They not only padlocked it, they welded the door shut. They're trying to starve us out."

"I don't think they'll be back for a while."

"Let's figure out what to do next. Do you recall any other ducts that access the cell area?"

"Did they close off the cell area?"

"Yep." Boone replaced the bar in its slot. "They did it right after they took you away to be revamped."

"I'll have to think about that. I know there's ventilation in every room, so there must be other ways to enter the main building."

"Let's map out the main building and see what we come up with," Boone advised. "I need to rescue Joe."

Dallas drew a detailed sketch of the main compound and placed an X where he remembered seeing outside ventilation covers. "Wait a minute. Seems like they sealed every one of the covers."

"You're kidding."

"No, but" — Dallas paused and then looked at his wrist. Below his wrist there was a slit. "There's a key that slides out of this hole. I'm not sure if I can make it do that, now that I'm disconnected from the main line. Check under your wrist, you should have one, too."

Boone turned his hand palm up and found it. Dallas closed his eyes and concentrated. The opening expanded and a narrow key glided out. As soon as he opened his eyes, it retreated.

"What did you think about to get it to come out?"

"I tightened my lower arm."

Boone extended and flexed his arm. The key flowed out, and Boone grabbed it. "Easy enough."

Taylor twisted and turned his arm, but nothing happened.

"You might not be equipped with a key. Let me look."

Taylor extended his arm.

"Nope," Dallas said. "I don't see one on you."

"Hmmm. Go figure. Are you ready, Taylor?"

"Wait. You're not going to leave me here alone, are you?"

"That's the rules," Boone stated. "We always leave someone behind in case we're captured."

"I don't know anything about what you have been doing here. Give me a run down first."

"We have decided to stop rescuing new bullies who are delivered to the compound, or we'll never be able to find a way home. But we need to recover Joe and this core group in the event that any of us are captured. Now that we know that the helmet is the mainframe of control, we'll try to remove that if we are revamped."

"I don't think it's a good idea to leave me here, guys. It would take more than one of us to help someone escape."

"Maybe Dal's right," Taylor said. "Maybe I should remain behind."

"I'm good with that. Are you ready?"

"As ready as I'll ever be."

Dallas convinced Boone to go up the manhole ladder closest to their cubby. There was no sound in the alley when they raised the cover, so it was easy access out of the tunnels.

"I can't tell where we are."

Dallas waved two fingers and advanced toward the intersection of four buildings with Boone close behind.

Does the sun never shine here? Boone thought.

They jogged to original vent cover, only to find that it was locked and welded shut. Dallas led him to another wing off of the same building and stopped at the next cover, but it left them too exposed, so Boone jogged around the corner where the next vent was under the cover of darkness. Boone was relieved to find this vent was only locked. He turned to talk to Dallas but he was nowhere to be found.

"Halt, hu-man!" he heard from the other side of the building.

Boone stiffened, thinking someone had seen him, then heard Dallas speak. "Where'd you come from?"

"Are you not DAL1931?"

"No, dweeb." The sound of a fist hitting a face echoed to where Boone stood.

Boone didn't waste any time working the vent cover. He twisted his arm to eject the key, but in his panic, the key wouldn't expel.

Humbots stomping from other directions made Boone's heart race. Dallas was putting up such a fight that it placed all the guard's attention on him. The key finally ejected, and Boone grabbed it, only to drop it. He plunged to the ground and felt around. *Why does my clumsiness have to rear its head at the worst possible time?*

More humbots passed the section of the building where Boone was, hurrying to detain Dallas. Boone found the key and clutched it. Sliding his hand along the edge, Boone shoved in the key when he found the hole. The cover released, allowing him to jump inside. He leaned against the wall and listened to Dallas being beat. From the sound, it was taking many humbots to subdue him.

Boone closed his eyes and shook his head. Dallas must have heard the humbots coming and sacrificed himself to keep Boone free.

There was silence, and then the humbots proceeded past the vent, carrying Dallas away.

With head hung low, Boone advanced through the shaft. This time he explored each room that was lit behind the vent covers that he passed.

The first room was full of younger humbots who stood at attention with their hands over their hearts, singing a song about the greater good of the Robotics Center.

When Boone approached the next crossing that went to a different area of the building, he decided to find out why a room was so intensely lit that the rays of light reflected clear to the intersecting ducts. He was hesitant to get near enough to observe through the slats, until he realized all heads were down.

Doctors dressed in surgery garb were standing around Sawyer, connecting the tentacles of the helmet to his brain. The eye in the middle of the helmet was no longer red, but blue as the other humbot guards.

"It is complete." Boone heard someone say.

His friend was no longer human.

Boone crawled backward to the intersection and leaned up against the duct wall. *Is this a hopeless cause? We free one kid, and two more are captured.* And yet none of them could find a way home without the other.

The humbots were efficient at singling out each child and transforming them into a collective force against bullying.

It was a sickening way to demonstrate to Boone how he had been singling out the weaker kids to take out his frustrations. Although converting his victims to become a bully had never occurred to Boone. When he paused to consider why he was locked inside this nightmare, it overloaded his ability to reason.

Please, God, if You're there, let this nightmare end right now. I promise to never intentionally hurt another person in my entire life.

A noise farther down the duct snapped Boone out of his self-reflecting. He crawled toward the sound finding a dimly lit room that was now quiet.

Boone peeked through the cover and saw Joe on a bed. There were two other girls lying on beds to his right. Boone's fist tightened after examining Joe's helmet. It was blue. *They sure didn't waste any time finishing the process on him.*

Joe rolled over, opened his eyes, and faced the ventilation cover. Boone moved away from the slats, watching for any other movement. Joe sat to swing his legs off the gurney. The door opened, and two guards came in. Joe pointed to the vent but couldn't talk. The guards gathered Joe and ushered him to the door. Joe kept looking at the vent until the door closed.

An urgency to get to Taylor thrust Boone toward the outside vent. He didn't know how long it would take Joe to communicate that they needed to check the ducts. He only hoped that Joe had not disclosed their new cubby location.

Boone replaced the outside cover and fumbled with the key in his hand. *Come on, Butterfinkle. A more fitting name would be Butterfingers.* Finally he turned the key and heard it lock.

Hopelessness covered him like a black cloud. He barely shifted into the shadows before a small squadron passed the alley entrance.

Why did it feel like twenty pounds of weights were attached to each leg? Boone constantly looked over his shoulder as he rushed to the nearest manhole cover. He swore he was being followed. *Is anywhere really safe?*

When Boone stepped into the confines of the canal, it felt like the mud in the middle of the tunnel had suddenly grown vines to entangle him, so he walked on the edges where the path was dry.

It didn't seem to make his journey any easier. Memories started flooding his mind.

Help! I can't swim! Someone – elp m – !

Boone turned to look behind, as those words seemed to call from the depths of the tunnel.

"Hey, dude, did you hear what happened to Dexter Ralston?"

Boone's heart skipped a beat. "No, what?" he tried to sound casual.

"He's in the hospital in a coma. They found him in the Lincoln Street irrigation canal."

"What happened?"

"At first they thought he just fell in somehow, but everyone who knows him says that Dex is terrified of going near the canal because he can't swim.

Then the docs said it looked like someone tried to rip his hair out, because they found blood on the top of his head. Do you know anything about it...do you know anything...do you know...?"

Leaning against the wall, Boone pressed his hands into his temples. It seemed impossible to stop the voices from the past.

Why were you stalking Brianne? Do you realize how serious stalking someone is? I was stalked by a boy in college who wouldn't take no for an answer. When a girl says no, respect that!

"I'm so sorry, Mom. What am I going to do when I get back to you?" Tears blurred his vision. "I've hurt you with what you know I've done, God help you when you find out the rest."

The clanging of a manhole covers returned his thoughts to the present. He pushed away from the wall and moved quickly to the bars.

When Boone tried to grip the loosened bar, it was like someone has re-cemented it. It didn't budge. He touched the bar next to it and it moved.

Get it together, Boone!

The sound of footsteps approached the last curve. Boone lifted the bar, slid through, and replaced the bar as he saw the arm of one guard appearing. Boone took one large step and dove for the passage, then crawled to the cubby's foyer. His breathing was heavy. Had he been too noisy?

The cubby door glided open, and Boone felt strong arms pull him inside. Boone cupped his hand over Taylor's mouth. They closed the entrance door and sat in the recesses of the living room...waiting.

The whole time they spent staring at the entrance door, not one sound was heard in the tunnel. Boone motioned to Taylor to follow him to the bunk beds.

They sat next to each other, and Taylor whispered, "What happened?"

"Dallas sacrificed himself to keep me safe. He put up quite the fight. They've totally revamped Joe and Sawyer, so I imagine Dallas is under total control again."

"Did they follow you?"

"I heard them behind me, but I wonder if I imagined that now. I think I'm going crazy." Boone ran his fingers through his hair.

"You look whipped, Buddy. Let's try to rest and deal with this tomorrow.

CHAPTER 15
A Desperate Prayer

———∿∿∿———

Boone found Taylor in the kitchen making breakfast.

"Are you feeling better today?" Taylor pulled out a chair. "Have a seat."

"Sorry, Taylor. I was a mess last night."

"It seems like the whole robotic nation is bound to find you and revamp you. I think they see you as the one who has put a kink in their normal flow of operations." Taylor placed pancakes, scrambled eggs, and juice next to Boone. "Do you realize that you have taken on the weight of finding a way home for all of us?"

"Not by choice. It just happened."

"Well, it's time to start delegating some tasks, my friend." Taylor lightly tapped Boone's shoulder as he sat to eat. "I think we should try to remove the helmets from Sawyer, Joe, and Dallas. That seems to be the way to free them from the mainframe of the control center."

"I don't know if it's a good idea for both of us to leave. If they capture us, there's no hope for anyone."

"There's really no choice because it'll take both of us to remove the helmet. Have you noticed that the humbots' tendencies don't lean toward aggressiveness?"

"They have come into the cells carrying rifles before, but they never really used them," Boone agreed. "However, Dallas had a new laser weapon that flashed from his third eye when Sawyer and him tangled."

"Oh. That's not good if they're straying from their regulation of non-aggressive behavior. "

Boone shoved his plate away. "We'll just have to attack when Sawyer, Joe, and Dallas are off guard. I studied Dallas's helmet before Sawyer took it. There's a latch under the chin and three areas around the perimeter of the skull that snaps off. It will take both of us to dismantle it. One of us will have to unlatch the chinstrap, and the other will have to bump it to disconnect it.

"I think we need to lure them to the tunnels. They walk through several times a day, that shouldn't be hard to do."

"True, but how do we separate them from each other so we can reach them one at a time?" Taylor collected their plates.

"And how are we going to get them back to the cubby? Dallas was pretty disoriented after his helmet came off."

"It's a matter of setting up a trap right around the bars."

"I think we should set the trap where the first hideout was. It will keep them away from the cubby."

"That could cause a problem if we can't get them back to the cubby before more guards make their rounds." Taylor wiped the plates and stored them.

"The two of us should be able to drag one of them here if they are immobilized. I'm not too good at figuring out ways to trap someone."

"I've got an idea that might work. We need some string and some old cans." Taylor started digging through the garbage.

"I grabbed a sewing kit on the last run to the supply room."

"Okay, let's gather some supplies in a pack and rescue one of our buddies." Taylor found eight empty cans. "I want to see if I can tap into a helmet and figure out if they have any knowledge of where the exit point is out of this world."

"So we only need one of them to find that out."

"Exactly. Preferably Sawyer." Taylor loaded the cans into a pack.

"Why Sawyer?"

"He's been with them the longest and observed the most. Even though he's only been partly functioning as a humbot, he should have more information downloaded."

"What happens if they don't program that information on the off chance that he would defect?" Boone finished packing the supplies.

"I don't even want to think about that." Taylor slipped the pack over his shoulder. "Let's go."

They weaved through the tunnels and knew they were approaching the first hideout by the putrid smell. The supply of rats was in abundance, as well. They either crushed them by hand or stomped them under foot. Before the rodent completely died, a mob of rats scattered to feast upon their fallen comrade.

"Dang." Taylor scooted around the feasting rodents. "Don't fall, or you'll become rat food."

"They might create another challenge for us when we disarm Sawyer. Here's the crevice to the other hideout."

"Okay, let's go a few yards farther past and set up a distraction that will separate them. Hopefully they only send two at a time, or this isn't going to work."

Boone held the flashlight as Taylor went to work. He took a spool of thread and doubled the strand, then punctured a hole on the top part of each can to string a cluster of four cans.

"Here, take this." Taylor handed Boone the cluster. "Go to the light we just passed and drape this over it. Take this spool, and run a double thread back here."

Boone walked about fifty feet and did as Taylor instructed. It was at a point where the tunnel curved, so Boone couldn't see Taylor. When Boone returned with the line, Taylor yanked it, and the cans clanged. It sounded a lot farther down the line than it actually was.

Taylor looped another line into the end of the cans and then hooked it around cracks in the cave wall. He attached the end to the opposite wall, allowing the thread to skim the top of the murky water flowing down the channel.

"What happens if something catches it as it comes down the canal?" Boone asked.

"Let's hope that doesn't happen."

"What happens if they come from the other direction?"

"They have always come from farther up the line, so I'm assuming they still will. When they go through the first set of threads, they'll both move toward the cubby. When they hit the second one, they'll split up to check out both of the rackets. We'll be waiting for the one who moves toward the compound."

"What will we do when the other cyborg comes back?"

"I'm hoping that we'll have one disabled and take down the other one when he comes to investigate."

"I don't have a good feeling about this." Boone scratched his head.

"I gathered that from the questions you've been asking."

"If you haven't noticed, they seem to always have the upper hand!"

"By dealing with them down here, they're out of their element. We can surprise them," Taylor reassured him. "Above ground, there are too many of them if something goes wrong."

"Okay, let's do this."

When they completed the last trap, they found a crevice where they could hide as the humbots walked past. The gap was only big enough for one of them, so Taylor had to go farther to find another fissure.

They waited for what seemed like hours and just as Boone predicted, a piece of wood snagged the line and brought the first set of cans crashing down. As they finished restringing it, they heard feet sloshing through the canal.

It was eerie watching the two humbots pass, Joe being the first, with Sawyer close behind.

Joe's foot disrupted the first set of cans, and they stopped as if someone turned off their switches. Joe motioned for them to continue, and Sawyer followed as Joe scrambled forward. When Joe's foot hit the second string, which jingled the cans behind them, they paused again, with both heads scanning up and down the tunnel.

Sawyer ordered, "You go ahead, and I will take the one behind us."

Boone stepped behind Sawyer as he came around the bend and slipped his hand under Sawyer's neck. The chinstrap easily snapped apart. Taylor quickly approached Sawyer from the front when the helmet slid over Sawyer's eyes, then used his palm to thrust the helmet backward. Sawyer went limp. Boone caught him and dragged him to the crevice he had come from.

Turning to where Joe had gone, Boone rushed forward to a darkened area of the tunnel and worried when he didn't see Joe. Boone stumbled, falling over Joe who was facedown in the puddle. Boone raced to flip him over, then dragged him away from the water.

"No!" Taylor shouted. "I won't go with you!"

"Release SAW1958!" A droid commanded.

Boone rushed toward the skirmish but skidded when he got to the corner. He watched two humbots grab Sawyer and yank him out of Taylor's arms.

Taylor swung his leg at one humbot, making him lose his balance, which caused the humbot to cascade on top of Taylor. Sawyer's deadweight pulled the other robot into the heap. Taylor was trapped beneath a pile of cyborgs trying to get free.

Reed stepped over his fallen companions and reached for Taylor's neck and squeezed. Taylor went limp. Reed pointed in Boone's direction as his comrades untangled.

Scurrying back into the crevice, Boone scooted along the darkened gap and went as far as he could. Boone kept an eye on the entrance and paused when he saw the humbots go by. It was difficult to steady his breathing as his heart thundered. Boone moved to the other side of the wall, going deeper into the cranny, praying that he would find another gap in the wall. To Boone's amazement, it felt like the wall opened, so he stepped into the black.

It wasn't long before two of the humbots entered the crevice. The third eye from their helmet efficiently lit both sides of the wall. Something moved to Boone's boot then scratched at his leg. Beads of sweat trickled down his back as the patrol approached.

The light shined directly into the fissure he was in, but noise farther down the gap drew the patrol's attention. The rat that had been clawing at Boone's leg was now making its way up his midsection. He didn't dare crush the vermin fearing that it would give him away.

Boone heard stomping, and then a squeal.

"Rats," one of them said.

The two humbots rapidly returned to the entrance. All of them congregated to discuss Joe's mishap. Two of them went to assist Joe, and the others went back to apprehend Taylor and revive Sawyer.

"The renegade hu-man must be farther down the tunnels." Two other robots went in the direction of Boone's cubby.

The rat was now on Boone's shoulder and sniffing in his ear. He could feel its teeth gently nibbling on his lobe. It was silent now. Boone reached up and crushed the pest. He lowered himself on his haunches and waited for the other two guards to return from the cubby area.

The sloshing of the water from the guards passing made Boone open his eyes. He couldn't believe he nodded off. Eager to get back to safety, he edged his way to the entrance and looked both ways.

All was quiet.

It felt like his heart refused to beat. Devastation was a cruel master of depression. Boone stepped into the tunnel as if his was wading through sludge up to his knees.

You have to keep going, Boone. You are their only hope.

He wasn't sure if he was talking to himself or if some unseen force was trying to offer a speck of encouragement.

What can I do to help? I've failed at everything I've tried.

The next thought was clearly not his own. *Just keep believing.*

Boone was never more relieved to see the bars that kept the humbots away from his safe haven. He mechanically removed the bar and replaced it. The closer he got to the cubby's entrance, the heavier his heart became.

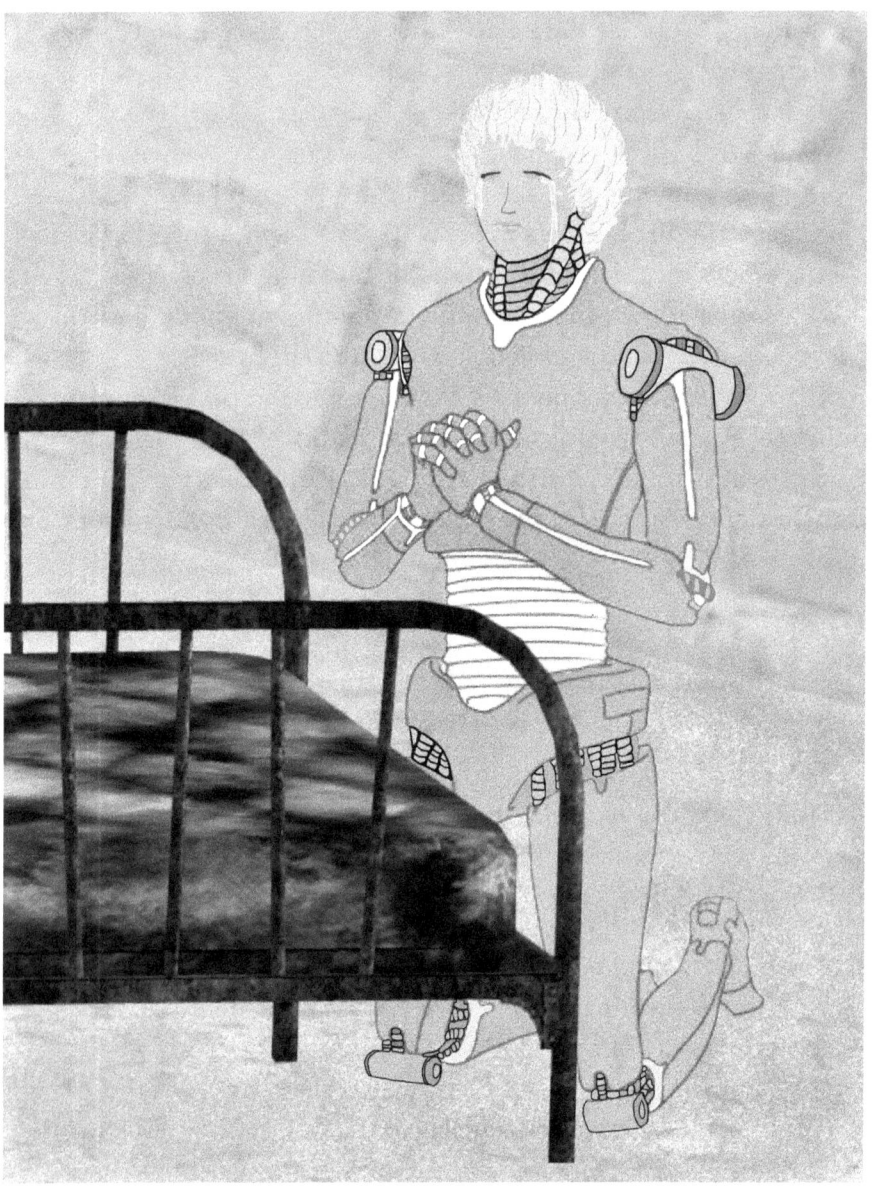

Through this whole experience, the time alone was the worst part. Boone finally made it to the first bunkroom and sagged by a bed.

Tears freely flowed. He couldn't remember crying this much since he was a child. Who could he turn to? Where could he go?

"Oh God," Boone muttered as he folded his hands. "Oh, Lord."

Boone shot up when he realized what he was saying. "It's You. I haven't prayed to You since I was a little boy. My parents believe, and I have never really cared. Why should You care what I have to say now? Now that I'm in trouble?"

Boone couldn't understand it, but he felt a warmth flow through him. *Oh yeah, I remember. That warmth was there when I talked to You as a boy.*

A faint smile graced Boone's lips. "I'm sorry, God, that I've forgotten about You. By the warmth I feel, I can tell You haven't given up on me." A wail escaped Boone's throat.

"Help me, Lord. I don't know what to do anymore. I want to go home. I want to help the others, but nothing I do works. Help me, Lord. Please help us."

Boone's words gave way to sobs. Peace, covering him like a warm blanket disrupted his anguished soul.

CHAPTER 16
Back At The Barbershop

Logan didn't notice anyone coming up the outside boardwalk to his barbershop, because his head was bowed in prayer. He glanced at the clock, not believing that only fifteen minutes had gone by. It was Brianne Watchler.

"Hi, Mr. Payne." She pranced in.

"Well, look at you." Logan smiled. "To what do I owe this privilege? When did you get your new look?"

"Oh, about two weeks ago." Color rose to Brianne's cheeks. "I'm not used to the attention it's drawing."

"I imagine the boys are discovering there's a Brianne now. God wired us to notice pretty girls."

"My dad wants me to go back to my geek look. I think it's silly that boys never noticed me before and now they do, when I'm the *same person*."

"Yeah, most of us men will admit that our standards are pretty shallow. So what can I do for you today?"

"I was just riding by and saw that you weren't busy. You've always been my favorite Sunday School teacher."

"Well thank you. That's the nicest thing I've heard in a while."

"I have a song to sing in the Memorial Concert this Friday, and I was wondering if you would like to go?"

"Absolutely. I wouldn't miss it."

"Oh, great. My folks are having a get together afterward. You can come to that too."

"I'd be honored."

Brianne tilted her head as she looked at the barber chair. "You know, I've never sat in a barber chair before. This one is cool because it looks ancient... not that you are ancient."

"Of course not. Feel free to sit in it."

Brianne snuggled into the chair and ran her finger over the worn brown leather that covered the arms. "This is way different than the beauty salon chairs. Who was your last haircut?"

Logan glanced at the ceiling where Boone had disappeared. "Boone Butterfinkle."

Brianne soared out of the chair and wiggled as she squealed, "Ooh, I don't like him!"

Logan's eyebrows arched. "Oh, why not?"

"He's been almost stalking me since I made my transformation. He locked Remmie Christensen in the storage room so he couldn't dance with me. I wasn't even at the dance. I was sitting with Dexter Ralston at the hospital. I heard that Boone bought all of my dance tickets, and when my mom and I left the hospital that night, one of my car tires had the air let out of it. I just bet Boone did that. I wouldn't doubt if Boone had something to do with Dexter, too." Brianne took a breath.

"Well, that is a lot not to like about a fellow. I heard about Dexter. He isn't out of his coma?"

"No." Brianne frowned. "The doctor said the longer that Dex is in the coma, the worse it looks for him."

"Why do you suspect Boone has something to do with Dexter?"

"I don't know. It's just a feeling I have." She settled down and went back to the barber chair.

"Feelings can lead you astray, Bree."

"Oh, I know," Brianne said with a huff. "I just don't like Boone. He's so ratchet!"

"Pardon me?"

"Another word for rude and obnoxious."

"Thanks for keeping me in the loop of new slangs."

"You're welcome." She tapped the chair arms. "So how high does this chair go?"

Logan stepped back as he gasped. The look on his face startled Brianne.

"Did I say something wrong?"

"Uh." Logan stepped in front of Brianne. "No. Um…you know, Brianne, you don't know what Boone is going through to make him act the way he does."

"I know. It's just that computers are way more predictable then boys."

Logan snickered. "I guess it depends on who you are."

"No offense, Mr. P. I know you were a boy once. But now you're a man, so it's different."

"Not by much," Logan said under his breath. "You still need to give him a little leeway. His genes are out of control right now."

"Just as long as he stays away from me, I will be all happy." Brianne patted her lap. "Now are you going to show me how high this chair goes?"

Logan's expression went blank. Today was the first time in ten years that anyone had ever asked that question. Now two within thirty minutes of each other asked—what were the odds? And what did Brianne need to learn? But who was he to doubt God?

Logan walked to the back of the chair to step on the hydraulic lever. "Okay." *Please stop where you normally stop.*

The chair steadily lifted and hesitated. Logan held his breath then let it out as the chair continued on. *Dear Lord.*

"Wee!" Brianne squealed like a little girl. But as the chair approached the ceiling, she quit. "Okay, Mr. P, you can let me down now."

"I'm sorry, Brianne. I don't know why, but God wants to teach you something. You will be all right. I—at least, I hope you will. Of course, God wouldn't let anything happen to you." Logan continued to talk even though Brianne was talking at the same time.

"Stop!" A mist fell upon them as the ceiling bubbled out. It was like the ceiling broke open. This time, Logan tried to see where the chair was going before it disappeared.

When Logan could no longer see Brianne, he staggered back to the waiting room and sank into a chair. His legs were shaking as the barber chair lowered without Brianne.

"Dear God, I know You're a God of many wonders. I don't understand what You're doing, but please let these children come back quickly and safely."

The phone rang, sending Logan into the air. He answered as casually as he could. "Payneless Barbershop, this is Logan."

"This is Betsey, Logan."

"Oh, hi, Betsey." Logan's voice was unusually high.

"Is Boone still there?"

"He just stepped out for a second." Logan bit his lip.

"Would you tell him that he'll have to walk home and to mow the lawn? I can't leave school yet."

"I sure will."

"Okay, thanks."

Logan walked around the barber chair as he moaned. That was one seat that he did *not* care to sit in.

"This isn't funny, Mr. Payne!" Brianne couldn't see the barbershop at all.

The chair stopped and the mist evaporated. She looked down and found herself dressed in a surgeon's smock covered by a lab coat. The doors of an elevator appeared before her. Rather then greet what was on the other side of the door while sitting in the barber chair, Brianne scrambled behind.

"What the hey is going on here?"

The doors parted, and two men and a woman with painted smiles waited for Brianne to move off the elevator. When she didn't, the woman extended her hand as she walked through the barber chair and grabbed Brianne's hand.

"Welcome, I'm Dr. Stein and this is Dr. Jankel and Dr. Hydener. We've been waiting for your arrival."

Dr. Jankel extended his hand as Brianne stepped off the elevator. "You are Dr. Watchler, I presume."

"Um." Brianne leaned away from their overwhelming attention. She glanced at a gold tag that was pinned above her right breast. It read, *Dr. Watchler*. "Where am I?" Her voice raised two octaves.

A group of children dressed in the most realistic robot costumes she had ever seen strolled by and waved at her.

"Did I miss the memo? Is this Halloween in May?"

The doctors stopped and stared at her.

"You know, like Christmas in July?" Brianne looked between the three of them as she wrung her hands. She didn't usually chatter like this because she was rarely nervous, but this unexpected turn of events sent her over the edge. "That would make Thanksgiving in June, wouldn't it?"

None of the doctors responded.

"Okay, forget what I just said." She looked down and shook her head.

Dr. Hydener ignored everything Brianne had just spewed and said, "Let's take you down to surgery right away so that you can observe our procedures."

Okay, I'll just play along.

"So how long have you been studying robotics?" Dr. Stein asked.

"Ever since I attended Hobbs Middle School?" Brianne answered in a question.

"They are that far advanced there?" Dr. Jankel said. "Impressive."

The doctors escorted Brianne to a room with a large window overlooking three different surgery rooms. There were nine other people who were already seated and ready to watch. Only one chair was left in the front row. Brianne picked up the pen and notepad on the chair and sat.

The boy next to her looked about sixteen-years-old. He extended his hand and said, "Just call me Doogie."

Brianne tilted her head trying to place where she had met him, then extended her hand. "Brianne Watchler. Nice to meet you."

"Likewise. It's an honor to be chosen. You'll understand soon." He turned his attention to the doctors entering their surgery rooms.

Brianne's gasped when she looked from room to room.

"Thank you for coming to this seminar," Dr. Jankel said from surgery room 1. "As you have been informed, you will learn in three easy steps how to deprogram the bully nature so prevalent on Earth through robotization. This high school girl will have both legs fitted and computerized within ninety minutes. A week ago, it took us several procedures to do what can now be completed in one day."

Dr. Hydener, who was standing in surgery room 2, continued, "And likewise, the upper torso can be finished within two hours the next day."

Brianne's stomach churned as she viewed the parts lined up against the wall to be assimilated on the child lying on the surgery table.

"And, Dr. Watchler," Dr. Stein said from surgery room 3. "This is where your expertise will be implemented: assembling the computer module in the helmet to permanently adhere to the brain, which will entirely eradicate all bully tendencies."

There didn't seem to be much of the child left in that surgery room. Brianne took a deep breath to stop her head spinning.

"And now we begin." Dr. Stein joined the other doctors in surgery room 1. "Pay close attention because we need more surgeons as soon as possible."

Brianne closed her eyes and prayed that she would be in Mr. Payne's barbershop when she opened them. Brianne looked at the same surgery rooms, tears brimming. She would not be returning to the barbershop — at least not for a little while.

CHAPTER 17
In Training

After the initial shock of being thrust into some kind of imaginary world, Brianne watched each phase of the surgery with fascination. They integrated all body parts with a platinum based material and stainless steel joints, which attached to the child's hip and arm sockets. The doctors said that it took a while to configure the perfect balance of materials not to be rejected by the human part of the subject.

Even though it enthralled Brianne to learn a new realm of robotization, the thoughts kept nagging her, *what purpose does all of this have? And why am I here?*

The doctors stopped the training after the second segment of the upper torso had been completed on a sixteen-year-old girl. They escorted all the interns to their individual quarters, which were lavishly furnished.

When Brianne entered her apartment, she wondered how they knew what her dream-come-true living space would be. A chair with elegant curves of cherry wood and ivory trellis upholstery sat in the center of room decorated in a traditional style, with molding accentuating the walls. A suede leather couch set on the other side of the cherry wood end table, draped by a hand-quilted comforter.

Even though the style of the apartment didn't look modern, the kitchenette had a device installed in the wall labeled Food Processor.

All Brianne had to do was say the meal she desired and a timer would alert its completion. *Welcome to a Star Trek episode, Bree.*

"Chicken cordon bleu with steamed broccoli, mashed potatoes with chicken gravy, and cinnamon apple sauce." The device counted down from five minutes.

Two tall-upholstered chairs were underneath a granite bar, so she sat and looked at her notes while she waited for the timer to go off.

Brianne remembered looking at Logan as the barber chair almost touched the ceiling and heard him say, "God wants to teach you something."

Why would God want to teach me robotics? Does He actually have a calling in robotics? This makes no sense.

The timer went off, and she eagerly went to the processor. The perfection of its display looked like it came from a high-class restaurant.

"Sparkling grape juice." Brianne said. In ten seconds the timer rang and she had her drink.

The spices in the food were like no other she had ever tasted. Brianne didn't think she would ever eat enough, but when she finished the last portion of applesauce, she felt satisfied.

After cleaning up she thought, *Well, Brianne girl, it's time to explore and find out why you're really here.*

She went to the entry door and found it locked. Brianne frowned as she stepped back. *You people think you're going to keep me captive, you've got another thing coming.*

The kitchen was a perfect place to find an instrument to pick a lock. A baggy tie bundle was in the utensil drawer. Brianne took a handful of them to create a wire prong by sliding the wire out of the wrapper and twisting them together. She slipped the prong into her smock top, and then took the thinnest paring knife she could find. Brianne leaned against the door to hear if anything going on in the hallway. All was quiet.

The knife fit perfectly between the door and the doorframe. She slid it where the doorknob locked, and the door released. Brianne barely opened the door to peek out. Nothing was stirring. She entered the hall and went the same direction she came in. The first room was labeled Storage. The next one read Custodial.

The next four doors weren't labeled but locked. *What's behind door number six? Oh but wait. What do we have here? Dr. Sarah Stein. We have a winner.* She wiggled her wire prong and heard the lock click. The room was dimly lit and empty.

Brianne sat in the doctor's chair to get a better look at her desk items. There was some device that was recessed into the top of the desk. Brianne grabbed the desk to move closer and accidentally touched a button. The recessed area slid back, and a monitor came to the top. Brianne grabbed the remote control and pushed the first button labeled Outside Compound. The monitor displayed a world void of life. *Wow, don't be going there.*

Recorded Prospects was the next button. A list of alphabetized names appeared. Brianne hit the first name on the list Abigail, and watched a tomboyish gal about fourteen-year-old come off of the same elevator that Brianne did. Only there was no barber chair in her elevator, just a closet full of different colored overalls.

Robots took her to a holding cell, and that was the end of her video. Brianne clicked on the B list to see if her arrival had been recorded. As she scrolled down the names, she stopped at *Boone.*

Nah. It couldn't be. Then she remembered Mr. Payne saying that Boone had been his last haircut. *I might as well take a look.*

Brianne tapped on Boone's name and huffed. *It is Boone!* She pulled the chair all the way up to the desk. *Well, I'll be. The same barber chair and elevator.* She watched him pass out in the classroom and then taken to a recovery room. The next video showed Boone being prepped for surgery. Even though Brianne didn't like Boone, a twinge of compassion touched her heart as she watched him go through the first surgery.

The doorknob jiggled. Brianne touched the monitor button and watched it disappear. *Oh no, I didn't put the controller back!* She rushed to a door on her right. It was some kind of library. There was another entrance door that would let her out. Brianne listened to make sure whoever was coming in wouldn't be out in the hallway.

The office door opened, and Brianne heard Dr. Stein talking with someone. The library's entrance door was locked. Brianne emptied a plastic file folder and slid it between the doorknob and the doorframe. The sound of the lock releasing was sweet. She scurried to her apartment door. That door had automatically locked, so Brianne reached into her pocket for the prong.

A red light started flashing at Dr. Stein's door, soon followed by an emergency beeper.

Brianne's trembling hands were slick as she grabbed the prong. She crammed it into the lock and it ricocheted, landing at her feet. Wiping her hands on her lab coat, she clutched the prong, too anxious to check out the footsteps coming down an adjacent hall. Brianne jammed the prong into the lock and smiled when she heard a click. A guard appeared at the intersection of the hallway next to Dr. Stein's office, just as she entered her apartment.

The safety of the closed door helped Brianne relax until she heard someone approach her door and stop outside. She quietly went to the leather couch and snuggled into the furthest corner, her eyes never leaving the door. The shadow that lingered at the bottom of the door finally left.

Taking a deep breath, Brianne wrapped the comforter around, her mind racing with questions. *Am I here to rescue Boone? How cruel is that? After he stalked me and did those horrible things? God, why would You ask me to do such a thing?*

That unmistakable wooing of her Lord answered her questions. *It is because I love Boone. You must forgive him.*

"Yeah, right," Brianne said out loud. "I know You love everyone no matter what they do, and I know You ask us to love our enemies, but why Boone?"

There was no answer. Brianne went to her bedroom and snuggled into bed. Even though she wrestled with the fact that she was sent there to help Boone, she was relieved to understand what was going on.

Just before she drifted to sleep she said, "Yes, Lord. I will do what You ask."

CHAPTER 18
Discovering Why

———*∞∞∞*———

An alarm clock went off beside Brianne's bed. It didn't have the time on its face; it just flashed Classes Begin Soon. Brianne tried to hit a snooze button, but couldn't find it. Her level of frustration grew, trying to find the blasted button, which made her wide-awake. She switched the alarm off and went to take a shower.

The Food Processor made a great breakfast of a ham and cheese omelet, hash browns, wheat toast and a vanilla latte.

The door opened, and a guard entered. "Time for classes," its computerized voice said. Brianne grabbed her notepad and followed him. "Did you sleep well, Dr. Watchler?"

"Yes, very well, thank you. What is your name?"

"My name, ma'am?"

"Yes, surely they call you something."

"My identification is TAY1954."

"TAY? I wonder if that's short for Taylor. I'll call you Taylor, if that's all right?"

The robot stopped and tilted his head.

"Is everything okay?"

He turned to her. "That name, Taylor, sounds familiar. If you wish, Dr. Watchler, you may call me by that name. We shall continue now. We are meeting in the Monitoring Center."

They passed several surgery rooms without speaking. When Brianne saw a bulky steel door labeled Recovery Cells, she stopped.

Taylor continued several steps until he heard Brianne. "What's this for?" She touched the door.

"That is where the subjects recover after each procedure."

"Were you in there after your surgeries?"

"I have no recall of my surgeries. It is for our benefit not to remember. Shall we continue?" Taylor extended his hand to the direction they were going.

How convenient. Brianne didn't know how she was going to pull off doing surgeries on these children when they had been brought here against their will just because they were considered bullies. Then they were forced to forget who they were by becoming more mechanical than human. *Why?*

They went to the end of the hall, and then Taylor pointed for Brianne to go down a narrow stairway. When they finally reached the bottom after descending many stories, a landing widened into a foyer. The atmosphere had all the markings of a dungeon converted into a control room for monitoring everything that was going on in and out of the building.

"Welcome." Dr. Stein greeted her. "We are going to give your studies a break today and show you around the compound. We hope that you and the others will choose to stay after your internship. There is nothing more thrilling then creating an elite military force that will govern Earth in the near future."

Brianne nodded and moved to the back of the crowd. It took several minutes to digest what Dr. Stein had just said.

"Monitor 1 is located on the outer perimeter of the protective shell of our compound," Dr. Jankel said. "We have created a hostile environment outside the compound to prevent any escapes by our subjects. After a legion of one thousand humans has been revamped, they will be trained there so they are able to adapt to any adverse environments without breaking down."

"Where is this compound located?" a student asked.

"That is a well-kept secret," Dr. Stein answered. "This is so remote that most people don't know it even exists."

"But we are still on Earth, correct?" a female student asked.

"Of course," Dr. Hydener answered. "Now on monitor 2 we can see the first mile that circles the compound area. We had an escape attempt two weeks ago. Let's watch the outcome of that one, shall we?"

The video zoomed in on a body lying in the middle of sand. It was a girl. As the camera focused on the child, it was clear from the bloating and blisters on the body that the temperatures were extreme. Brianne watched the reaction of her fellow students. All were appalled.

Then a teen appeared on the monitor, who was robotized to his neck, and trying to climb a sheer rock wall. The boy kept looking down, and when the camera panned below, Brianne could see his concern. If he fell, he would be impaled by blades and jagged steel pieces that spiked the ground. The camera swept to the top of the cliff and showed the teenager climbing over the crest. His face was chapped from the severe weather. The video stopped in the middle of his capture.

One of the robots watching suddenly left the room. Brianne was certain that he was the boy who had been pursued and caught.

"Next is monitor 3," Dr. Stein said. "We just installed these yesterday. We have an escapee who has eluded us for over a week. He is somewhere in the tunnels below the compound. There was a small group who formed an offense against the compound. All of them have been completely revamped, except this one named Boone."

Brianne took a deep breath when the monitor projected Boone robotized to his head.

The next video was in the tunnels. Someone approached a guard from behind and unlatched the guard's helmet. Taylor, who hadn't been totally revamped, flipped the helmet off of the guard. Brianne's covered her mouth when she saw Boone catch the guard before he fell. Boone gently lowered him into Taylor's arms. The cans rattling farther up the tunnel sent Boone running in that direction. When he rounded a corner, there was no more video coverage.

"This boy," Dr. Stein's eyes narrowed as she clenched her teeth, "has thwarted our every effort to be captured. When he came to us, we marked him as the leader of our new nation. We have a plan in place. He will soon be captured."

There was no doubt that Brianne was the bait to capture Boone. Her pulse quickened as rage overwhelmed her. Black spots appeared in her vision, then she slumped to the floor.

"There, see," Brianne heard a computer-generated female voice. "She is coming around. She will be fine."

Brianne saw a robotic nurse leaving. Taylor sat across from her in the upholstered chair in her apartment.

"I am glad you are A-OK."

Brianne chuckled. Her dad used to say A-OK when she was little. It meant she was absolutely safe and secure.

"I didn't mean to cause such trouble." Brianne tried to rise.

Taylor put his hand on her shoulder. "Dr. Stein insists that you rest for the remainder of the day."

"Could you bring me some water, please?"

"I can do that." He went to the Food Processor and ordered ice-cold water.

Brianne gratefully accepted the water and noisily gulped it all. "That's best water I have ever drank."

"It sounded like it tasted good."

"Oh." Brianne blushed. "I'm sorry for my lack of etiquette."

"May I escort you to your resting room?"

"I can get there on my own."

"Then I will leave you to rest." Taylor turned to leave.

"Taylor? Do you know where that tunnel is we saw on the monitor?"

"Yes. I have been there many times."

"After I rest, could you take me there?"

"I have been programed to guide and protect you. I can take you there."

"Oh, thank you. Can you come for me in about four hours?"

"I shall return then." Taylor bowed and left.

Brianne sank into the couch and had no difficulty falling to sleep.

⚍

Boone went to the original hideout hoping to find Sawyer's helmet. After retracing his steps two times, he decided they must have taken it. He started for the cubby but stopped when he came to the intersection that joined with the tunnel to the first hideout. There were two voices: one was computerized and the other a human female.

Boone doused his flashlight and crept closer to hear what they were saying. The girl's voice was familiar, but he couldn't place it. The other voice was definitely Taylor's. Why was Taylor leading a girl to their first refuge?

"Do you think Boone ever comes here?" she asked.

"From the cameras we have set up, we have seen him coming and going. By the time we deploy guards, he is gone."

Has Taylor brought a prisoner down here? Boone wondered. *Why would she know me by name?*

"Where does he go? Which direction?"

"He heads farther down the tunnel." Taylor pointed.

"Okay, after we check this space, take me there, please."

"As you wish."

Boone couldn't hear them anymore as they entered the alcove of the hideout. This girl was giving orders to Taylor, and he was acting in a servile manner. That made no sense at all. It wasn't long before they returned. Risking all, Boone leaned around the corner as they entered the tunnel.

His mouth dropped open. *Brianne! How? Why?* Leaning against the alcove wall, he lowered his head. *This is over the top if she came here to get even!*

Boone ventured out and trailed them from a distance. Something spinning on a motorized axis drew Boone's attention above. Next to a dim light, a camera spanned the length of the canal.

Oh, we've been busy installing cameras, have we? Great! Boone paused in the shadow and waited for the camera to sweep the other direction. He wondered how many of those he had missed. With each bend in the tunnel, another camera rotated back and forth forcing Boone to hug the shadows of the walls. Fortunately, most of them hadn't been synchronized.

When he approached the cubby, cameras flanked both sides of the tunnel forty feet from where the bars were. One was swinging around as the other one just left his section. Boone jumped on a nearby manhole ladder to miss being detected. Brianne's voice sounded close, quickening Boone's steps upward.

"So you say they took a large part of the food, water, and supplies from this room? I wonder where they put it."

"That has been our dilemma. We welded the door shut until we realized that was another way to trap him."

"Oh, yes. Did we lock the supply door?"

"I will check." Taylor left her side.

Boone climbed down to see what Brianne was doing. She had something in her hand, walking along the wall and looking for something.

What is that she has? Boone checked both cameras and hopped down off of the ladder. *A note!*

A crack in the wall beside the last bar now housed a note. Taylor returned so Boone climbed to the top of manhole ladder.

"Can we go up this manhole?" Brianne asked as they approached it. Boone rolled his eyes.

"No. We will have to go down two more section to exit. We have barricaded these since they are so close to the storage room."

Thank God! Boone exhaled.

"Did this excursion help, ma'am?"

"Yes, I think so, Taylor."

"Will you help capture Boone?"

"I don't think they need my help." Brianne frowned.

"Is that not why you are here?"

"I thought I was brought here to be trained."

Taylor remained silent.

"Oh boy..." Brianne stared blankly.

When the sloshing of water ceased, Boone lowered himself into the canal and made a beeline to whatever Brianne hid.

Boone,

*This is Brianne. I don't know how this happened,
but I think I am here to help you escape. Would you
meet me at this time tomorrow right here? We'll
figure out how to get home.*

Brianne

Boone tightly clutched the note as he hurried to the cubby. His mind was whirling on why and how Brianne got thrown into this mess. *Why would she even want to help me after all I've done?*

Boone read Brianne's notes several more times. A shadow of hope grew in his heart, but then he thought, *what if this is a trap? Taylor and Brianne were friendly toward each other. But then she did have Taylor leave so she could hide the note. How did she get here? Did Mr. Payne send her here to find me? Or did she get here through some other channel? Or what if—.*

Boone shot to his feet and looked up. "Is this Your answer to my prayer, God? No way! Send someone else, like that Michael Archangel dude!"

CHAPTER 19
Finding A Game Plan

It was difficult sitting still as Boone waited for time to pass. He slept a couple hours and finally decided to find the perfect vantage point to see Brianne coming down the canal. Boone wrote a note and placed it where Brianne had deposited hers.

On the opposite side of the entrance there was an indention in the rock wall big enough to sit undetected while watching Brianne.

Splashing in the tunnel jolted Boone awake. Brianne stepped into the entrance of the storage room and disappeared. When she returned, she looked disappointed. Boone checked to make sure that no one else was with her. Brianne went to the storage room several times, then quickly moved to the place she had left her note and found Boone's. She glanced in both directions of the tunnel as she unfolded the note.

Brianne,

I can't believe you are here. Why are you? Are
they using you to trap me? If you come alone
tonight, I'll know, because I'll be watching.
Then I'll meet you tomorrow night at this
same place and time.

Boone.

Brianne leaned out of the entrance and loudly whispered while looking in every direction. "Boone, I'm here to help. Please come out. I don't..." Brianne stopped when she heard something farther down the canal. Maybe she wasn't alone. She produced another slip of paper and quickly wrote. She peered over her shoulder and then shoved it into the same crack.

Brianne started to walk away, but stopped to examine the area beyond the bars. After looking from one end to the other, she quickly retreated.

Boone kept hidden, listening for any indication of Brianne being followed. If she had, it appeared that she didn't know, because she looked startled when the drainage from the compound emptied into the canal. That noise alarmed Boone for days after he made these tunnels his home.

When Boone could wait no longer, he retrieved the note and slipped through the bars. Rushing to the cubby, he didn't care how much noise he made. Then with trembling hands he read:

Boone,

I don't know all of the whys, as I am sure you don't
either. I've forgiven you and I know without
a shadow of doubt that I am here to help you get
home. I know they are watching me. I'm trying to
not get caught. I don't know if I can come tomorrow
night. If I don't make it, keep returning until I do.

Brianne

"You stupid —!" Boone shouted. "Why didn't you trust her?"

It took Brianne several minutes to wrestle the manhole cover off and scoot it back on. Fortunately it was in the shadows and the compound entrance wasn't too far.

Brianne's apartment never looked so inviting when she closed the door. The stench of her boots and pants beckoned her to the bedroom where she shed them to step into a hot shower.

The fragrant lavender shampoo and the vanilla bath soap made her feel like she was home. She rolled her hair into a towel and wrapped a plush robe around. When she went into the bedroom, she leaped into the air at the movement on her bed.

"I don't have to ask where you have been from the smell that greeted me when I opened your door." Dr. Stein's pinched nose turned up. "You will need to dispose of those jeans."

"I wasn't aware that you could just barged into any apartment of your own choosing."

"We are aware of your connection to the subject, Boone Butterfinkle. We allowed your one excursion, but that will be the last one unattended."

"So I am here merely as a lure?"

"Primarily, but you have other redeeming qualities as well."

"And what if I refuse to help you?"

"We can always use another humbot." The evil smirk on Dr. Stein's face made Brianne shutter.

"Why is it so important to totally revamp Boone?"

"Each bully on Earth seals their own doom. The United Council determined three years ago that bully tendencies would be the perfect subjects for creating a militant race for a one-world government.

"We have to maintain strict community adherences with each child that is totally revamped. We allowed Taylor to show just enough humanness to trap you. He will no longer be your guard."

"Do you know how crazy you sound? What gives you the right to steal these children and destroy their lives so you can use them for your twisted plans?"

"Now that's not the kind of attitude I want to hear from you, or we will not be able to use you to capture Boone. You see, we have found an inner resourcefulness in Boone that few of the other subjects have. He will make a great general over the humbot race." Dr. Stein tightened her lips. "This is really in his best interest."

Brianne sneered at Dr. Stein then turned her back. Dr. Stein came behind her, placed her hands on Brianne's shoulder, and squeezed. Brianne stood her ground and didn't falter.

"Think on this, Miss Watchler. If you do not help us, we will start procedures on you in two days. We have no idea what these surgeries will do to a nonaggressive person."

Dr. Stein released her hold and left the room. Brianne heard the apartment door close, and collapsed to the floor. She lowered her robe and was surprised to see bruising already. While Brianne was on her knees, she lifted her voice to the only one she could.

"Father God, Mr. Payne said You want me to learn something through this experience. I can't even imagine what that might be. I thought it was because I needed to forgive Boone. I swear to You, I forgive him. If I am lying to myself, then show me. I need Your help, because there is no one else to turn to." Brianne bowed her head and cried when the reality of what she had just prayed hit home.

The next morning, Brianne forced herself to eat, even though she didn't feel like it. A knock on the door spiked her nerves so much that she almost lost the little she had eaten.

Brianne stepped back not expecting to find a six-foot-four cyborg darkening her doorway.

"My name is SAW1958. I will be your guide and protector." He extended his robotic arm stiffly to shake her hand.

Brianne looked into the humbot's warm brown eyes and hoped that the human kindness that was radiating from them would be the part that she could connect with to find a way home. "Is that short for Sawyer?"

"My name is..."

"May I call you Sawyer?"

The humbot hesitated, as if trying to compute what Brianne had asked. "That sounds familiar," he said, just like Taylor did. "You may call me Sawyer, Dr. Watchler."

"Only if you will call me Brianne." She smiled.

"I can do that." Sawyer moved out of the way. "Shall we go?"

Sawyer ushered Brianne to the observation room. The first session taught where to install homing devices: one under their left arm, and one behind the third eye. They discussed how many of the earlier humbots still only had one homing device under their arm. They began installing the second one after Boone dismantled several of their humbots' first devices.

During the second session, Brianne learned that all humbots had a button located on the right side of the neck underneath their ear that deactivated them for thirty minutes.

When classes ended, Dr. Stein met Brianne and Sawyer at her apartment door.

"Well, Dr. Watchler, what is your decision to help us find Boone?" Dr. Stein's said condescendingly.

"I have no choice as I see it. I will do it."

"Excellent. Meet me at my office tomorrow morning for details. SAW1958, keep watch at Dr. Watchler's door throughout the night."

"Yes, ma'am." He instantly stood in guard mode to the right of the entrance.

"Good night, my dear."

Brianne gladly closed the door, then rolled her eyes and mimicked the doctor, "Good night, my dear."

There was no time to waste. Brianne went to her closet and prepared an outfit of boots, jeans, and a jacket, but had to stop when someone knocked.

A different humbot stood at the door. It was a female.

"You are required to attend a banquet for the students. Please come with me."

"Right now?"

"Yes, now."

Brianne breathed in deeply and closed the door.

The banquet lasted all night. It was a presentation of benefits for a career at the Robotics Compound. Brianne was so drained of energy when she got to her apartment that she dropped into bed and didn't consider finding Boone.

It was in the middle of the night when Brianne woke - startled. She sensed that someone was in her room. There was no sound, only a presence.

"Who's there?" Brianne whimpered as she drew her blankets up to her chin.

A shadow went to the bedroom doorway and then left before a flash of a light flowed from the entrance of the apartment. Just as quickly as it had appeared, it went out.

Brianne backed into her pillow and covered her head with her blankets. She reached to turn on the table lamp as she peeked from the covers. Draping herself with a robe, Brianne tiptoed to the closet. From the faint glow of the lamp, she rummaged through a closet she had never explored, for anything to defend herself.

As Brianne bent over to get what appeared to be a cane, someone tapped her shoulder. She flew forward, slamming into the clothes hanging in the closet, which cushioned Brianne impact when she hit the wall. She bounced back, bottom first into the person behind her, sending them out of the closet. Grabbing the closet door, Brianne slammed it shut with her inside – alone – in the dark.

She couldn't believe it when she heard knocking on the door. Something moved behind Brianne, grazing her arm.

"Aaah!" She pressed toward the door.

Then another knock. Brianne staggered backward.

"Who's out there?" She half cried, half shouted. "I have a — a weapon." She lowered herself to the floor groping for the cane but couldn't find it, so she pointed her index finger and curled the rest of them before shoving her hand into her bathrobe pocket.

"It is I. SAW1958."

"Oh, for crying—" Brianne yanked open the door. "Are you the one who was in my bedroom a minute ago?"

"The entrance door opened. I thought you might need assistance. I did not know they issued weapons for your protection."

Brianne brought her hand out of her pocket, pointing her finger. "Bang, bang."

Sawyer leaned to look at her hand.

"Never mind." Brianne stepped out of the closet. "I could use your help, now that you're here."

"Yes, ma'am."

"I need that cane down there."

Sawyer bent over enough for Brianne to reach the right side of his neck. She jammed her fingers under Sawyer's right ear and heard gears coming to a halt. Sawyer leaned forward with his back still bent and stopped when his head hit the floor.

"Thank you, Robotics University, for teaching me how to disable a humbot." Brianne smiled as she reached down to take the scanning device on Sawyer's wrist, which gave him free access to any building in the compound. She draped her robe over his rump, which was the highest point of his body, and closed the closet door. Gathering the outfit Brianne had placed on the bed earlier, she quickly changed.

She swiped the scanner over her entrance door lock and heard it click. *How sweet is that?* Peeking into the hallway, the hairs on the back of her neck rose. Brianne glanced over her shoulder expecting the same shadow in her bedroom to be standing behind her.

"Forget this. I'm out of here."

She shut the door and raced to the end of the apartment complex until she came to an exit. There were concrete stairs, so Brianne hustled to the bottom. Using Sawyer's wrist badge, Brianne gained access outside.

There was a slight feeling of freedom, and yet she still had a long ways to go before she would be rid of this nightmare. There were many places to keep in the shadows as she made her way to the closest manhole that would lead Brianne to Boone. She just prayed that he would still be waiting for her.

Brianne sloshed through the flowing water in the middle of the canal until she realized there were cameras scanning the tunnel. Her sprint turned into strategic passage without detection to the storage room. *This is taking way too much time!*

When Brianne came to the last corner before the storage room entrance, she paused for a moment. There stood the shadow of someone pacing back and forth. It never occurred to her that it could be someone else. Brianne didn't slow her pace until she stood five feet in front of him. She slid to a stop when she realized this person was bigger than Boone.

Her heart was racing. How could she have been so foolish?

Then tears filled her eyes when she heard Boone's familiar voice, "Brianne?"

Brianne flung her arms around his waist and wouldn't let go.

Boone couldn't believe that Brianne, the girl he had tried everything to get to acknowledge him, was now hugging him. He just kept his arms to his side and then pulled away.

"Brianne, why are you here? Were you followed?"

"I don't know. I had to disable a humbot that was guarding me to make it here. They wanted me to set a trap for you."

"Okay, follow me." Boone grabbed her hand. He removed the bar and led her through, then swiftly took her to the cubby.

Brianne scanned the living quarters and shook her head. "What is this place?"

"Who knows? We figure it's been here for decades, and that's why the Robotics Center has it blocked off."

"Why haven't they looked for you here if they know it's here?"

"You're shaking." Boone ignored her question. "Let me get a blanket." Boone returned and draped a comforter over Brianne.

"Thank you."

"Let me make you something hot to drink."

Brianne took his hand and pulled him to the couch. "We need to talk. I don't know if I was followed. They've got cameras everywhere. I forgot that in the first part of the tunnels, so they obviously know I'm down here."

"Okay. You're right. How did you get here, Bree?"

"I went to Mr. Payne to invite him to my Memorial Day performance. I asked him how high his barber chair went. Before I knew it, I was in this weird world. Mr. Payne said you were the last one in his shop. How did you end up here?"

"I asked the same dumb question. I was hoping this was a dream, but when you arrived—what the heck are we doing here?"

"Mr. Payne said that I needed to learn something. I think I learned what I needed to, so why am I still here?"

"What did you need to learn?"

"To forgive you."

"You may not forgive me when you find out everything I've done."

"I don't think we have time to go over that now. We need a plan to find the exit to this place and get home."

"I entered on the barber chair in an elevator, but some others I talked to said they got here in different ways," Boone said.

"I entered the same way you did. I was so disoriented when I arrived here, I couldn't tell you where that entrance is."

"Same here."

"So why do you think you're here, Boone?"

"You know why I'm here." Boone stood and paced.

"Yes, but it would be refreshing to hear it from your lips."

"I'm a bully! Are you happy?" He sat down and lowered his head into his hands.

Brianne placed her hand on Boone's arm. "What an aggressive way to expose a problem."

"Unfortunately, bullies are extremely bullheaded, and it takes extreme methods to wake us up."

"Yikes. May I never be one. However, I was sucked into your nightmare, regardless."

Boone snickered. "Sorry about that."

"Let's see if we can get out of it." Brianne stood.

"I saw that Taylor escorted you to the first hideout."

"You know Taylor?"

"Yep, he was the one who helped me transition into the robotics after my first surgery."

"He's not my guard anymore since he guided me to the canals."

"Who's guarding you now?"

"I call him Sawyer. I left him deactivated in my bedroom closet. That's how I got here."

"I know Sawyer, too. He was another cellmate. How did you know how to deactivate him?"

"They are training me to be a surgeon. I learned it yesterday in class."

"That's too bizarre. So what are we going to do now?"

"One of the doctors gave me an ultimatum. Deliver you to them or become a humbot by the end of the day."

Boone quickly stood. "So this is your revenge!"

"Calm down, Boone. It just means that I can't go to the compound. By the time they see me running through the tunnels on the monitors, they'll know my choice."

Boone relaxed and sat. "I'm sorry. You have no idea what it's like to have these kids work beside you to free other kids and then they turn against you when they're revamped. You begin to trust no one."

"I can understand that. I find it hard to believe that I am trusting you when you were driving me nuts at home." Brianne's hand flew to her mouth. "Did I just say that out loud?"

"I deserve everything you have to say to me. So what's next? I've run out of plans."

"Well, I think the best place to find the exit point to this robot factory would be in the monitor room."

"I've been there more than once. It was always pretty well guarded."

"I heard Dr. Stein say to a group of students that this time of day has the least amount of guards. And if there is a breach where they need to deploy guards to that area, it will only have one guard."

"Do you think they've discovered that you're missing?"

"I would bet on it, so the sooner we get to the monitoring center the better chance we have to find our way out of here."

"Okay. Let's pack some provisions, and we'll be on our way."

CHAPTER 20
The Trap

Boone led Brianne to the manhole cover where he calculated the location of the monitoring center. As Boone climbed up the ladder, the clanging of other manhole covers being removed echoed to them.

"Hurry, Boone." Brianne shoved his back. "I think they're right behind us."

Boone lifted one side of the cover to look out. Humbots roamed every area of the compound. "Wow," Boone whispered. "I wish we had a cloaking device."

"Pretty bad, huh?"

Boone slid the cover to the ground, reached for Brianne and yanked her into his arms. Brianne's eye widen when she saw a patrol approaching. Boone carried her to the nearest shadow and lowered to the ground. The patrol circled the open manhole and entered one by one.

When they were gone, Boone realized he had never been to this alley. He motioned for Brianne to follow, but the alley dead-ended. Boone slapped his hand to his head. Brianne tapped him on the shoulder and pointed to a stairwell.

"That must be the back entrance to the monitoring center," Boone whispered. "How lucky is that?"

"Luck has nothing to do with it."

Boone raced down the long stretch of concrete stairs and stopped at the locked door. "Great. Do you know how to pick a lock?"

"Actually, I do, but we don't need it." Brianne showed Sawyer's pass.

"Wait a minute. They're probably monitoring all entry transactions."

"Good point. Don't you think an alarm will sound if I pick it open?"

"Another good point." Boone paused to think. "Okay, when we use Sawyer's pass, I'll disarm the guard inside, and then you find the monitor. I'll stand watch while you look."

"What do we do when we get caught?"

"Don't you mean *if*?"

"The odds are against us."

"I've always thought you were a possibility thinker," Boone said with a grin.

"It never hurts to have a plan." She faked a slug to his arm.

"Sorry, I shouldn't be teasing you when you're right. Well, this could go a hundred different ways. If they find us, we'll both be processed. All we can do is try to free each other and return to the cubby until we find a way home. I believe you'll find the location of that elevator."

"Okay, we can do this." Brianne slid the identification over the entry beam, and the door unlocked. Boone pulled a spray can out of his bag and opened the door slightly to glance in. It was the hallway to the backside of the monitoring room. He sprayed the camera lens after entering with Brianne close behind.

Boone nodded and painted the next two cameras. Another door stopped them at the end of the hall. Boone peeked through the narrow window to get an idea where guards were. One was standing just off to the right. He couldn't see if another guard was near. Boone motioned one, two, three, and rushed through the door. The guard slammed against the wall landing on his rump. Brianne finished the job by pressing the button below his right ear.

Boone took a closer look at the guard. "That's Reed. He's a good one to have out of commission."

"I'll get to it."

Boone faced the main entrance while Brianne glanced at each title above the monitor as she rushed through the room. When she got to the furthest wall, she stopped and sat. Just then, another guard appeared. It was Sawyer.

"You must come with me." Sawyer extended his arms.

"Sawyer, old buddy," Boone said, walking backward as he advanced.

"That does not compute."

"We helped kids escape from being revamped, don't you remember?"

"I belong to the Robotics Compound. You must be processed."

"You helped me when I first got here. We were cellmates."

"You have become an enemy of the cause."

Boone had finally run out of room because Brianne now stood next to him.

"Dr. Watchler, you deactivated me. You have become an enemy of the cause."

"Sawyer, we've got to fight this. This is evil." Brianne pounded her fist into her hand.

"What is evil?"

That stumped both Boone and Brianne. The revamping had erased all knowledge of right from wrong. Boone motioned for Brianne to go around the aisle of monitors to approach Sawyer from behind.

"Evil is wrong," Boone said.

"Evil is bad?" Sawyer tried to process within what the Robotics Center had programmed. "It hurts other people and things?"

"That's correct, Sawyer. Evil is very bad."

Brianne approached Sawyer's blind side, took two big steps and latched onto Sawyer's back.

Sawyer reached for Brianne's shoulders and flung her forward. Brianne slammed to the ground with such force that she didn't move.

Boone knelt next to her. "Bree, please be all right?"

Sawyer bowed down to look. "Is she alive?"

"This is evil, Sawyer. You have hurt her!"

"Good job." They both turned to the voice. It was a doctor with five guards behind her. "I'm Dr. Stein, and I have waited a long time to meet you, Boone. You have great things ahead of you."

"Stein, as in Frankenstein?" Boone glared at her. "Boy is that accurate."

"Take them."

"Take me, but leave Brianne alone!"

"She has outlived her usefulness now." Dr. Stein waved her hand. "She lured you to us."

"I swear." Boone clenched his teeth. "If you hurt her, I will be your worst enemy."

Dr. Stein cackled, then said, "And what can you possibly do to stop us?"

Two guards clamped on to Boone's arms and dragged him out of the monitoring room.

"Bree! I'll get you home! Just hang on!"

Two guards waiting at the top of the stairs with a stretcher brought Boone some comfort knowing they wouldn't immediately discard Brianne.

Boone stopped walking, forcing the humbots to drag him to the holding compound. He couldn't believe the transformation to the cells. Every area was closed off with steel walls and individual cells. They threw Boone in the middle. The only opening was an eighteen-inch by one-foot window with bars. Even if he ripped the bars out, he couldn't escape from these cells.

It was Boone's escape that had motivated such a fortified prison system. How unfortunate for the new bullies coming in. How unfortunate for him.

When the door slammed, a hollow echo rang throughout the cellblock. Boone heard the main entrance gate close, and he would have been good with the complete silence that usually followed after they left. Instead, what he heard crushed his heart. Cries from the surrounding cells pleaded for the pain to stop, or for the nightmare to end, or to just go home.

"Oh, God." Boone raised his hands over his ears. "Help us, please."

CHAPTER 21
Total Revamp

Dr. Stein followed the stretcher with Brianne to the recovery room and instructed a nurse, "Run a check on her. When she wakes, put her in the Immediate Total Revamp Program. She will be an excellent candidate for that experiment."

This would be the best acting job Brianne would ever perform; howbeit comatose was an easy role. Boone had given her enough time to find the exit point. Now she would wait for Boone to be brought in for prep work before his last surgery.

Brianne heard a doctor and a nurse discussing Boone's scheduled surgery for the following day. The Robotics Compound had such an influx of new bullies coming in that they moved Brianne to a room of rejected robot parts. It was an unguarded room and became part of the plan for their escape.

The dayshift workers woke Brianne out of a sound sleep. She hopped off the gurney just as Dr. Stein came through the door.

"Well, this couldn't be better timing!" Dr. Stein clucked her tongue. "We have Boone scheduled for completion this morning, and now we can start you on our ITR Program at the same time."

"The thing that baffles me the most is you don't even realize how sick you are."

"Au contraire, my dear, I am just very creative."

"Oh, is that how you choose to lie to yourself?"

"Nurse. Wheel her to the surgery prep room and give her a sedative drip at five milligrams."

"But, doctor, that could kill her."

"Very well, make it three. By the time she wakes, she will be totally robotic, and so will Boone."

The doctor walked out of the room, and the nurse went into the pharmacy to prepare the drug. Brianne took the tape off of the IV going into her vein, removed the IV, and placed a piece of gauze to catch the fluid. She resealed the tape and lay down.

The nurse returned and pushed all of the air out of the syringe.

"You don't have to do this, you know."

"It is an order." The nurse pushed the needle into the port.

The nurse put Brianne's arm under the cover and waited for Brianne to close her eyes. Brianne complied just to get the nurse to leave. Now all she had to do was wait for Boone to be wheeled in. Brianne moved the clamp under her sheet and shut off the IV hose.

The quietness of the room relaxed her as she settled into the gurney...waiting.

—∞—

It was the noise of a gurney being wheeled in that woke Brianne. She almost opened her eyes, but remembered where she was. When the room cleared, Brianne peeked to see if it was Boone then rolled off the gurney.

"Boone, are you ready? I know where to go."

He didn't move.

"Boone?" Brianne tapped him. She opened one of his eyes with her thumb. It was dilated. "Oh, man." She stomped her foot. She hadn't counted on him already being sedated. "Hang on. I'm removing your IV."

She stepped into the parts room and tore off her hospital gown. She borrowed a surgeon's pants, smock, and lab coat from the ready room. Brianne gathered as many robotic parts as she could and placed them on top of Boone. Then she covered Boone's head with the sheet.

Brianne stood on her toes to look in the recovery room window. "We are good to go." She unlocked the wheels of Boone's gurney, blazed through the double doors, past the vacant beds, and out the opposite end of the recovery room.

The maintenance staff made runs to the incinerator every so often to deplete their stock of damaged robotic parts. According to the map, Brianne had to pass the school to get to the incinerator. That's where the elevator was located to get home.

It was just a matter of time before a compound alarm would sound, when the nursing staff discovered that they were gone. Brianne was amazed that the gurney wheels could move as fast as she was pushing. Wind kept catching the bed sheet and flipping it up. Body parts were teetering toward the edge of the gurney.

It was six thirty in the morning, and the school wasn't operating. Brianne wondered how they would enter the building, when an opened utility door came into view. She leaned back and skidded with her feet. Boone started to come around and tried to rise.

"Don't move, Boone." Brianne leaned near his ear. "We're on our escape route. I need you to be quiet."

"Okay," Boone slurred and lowered his head.

A piercing horn blared.

"Could you turn off the alarm, Bree?" Boone giggled.

She slammed the utility room shut and wheeled the gurney in search of an elevator. There was one at the end of the darkened hallway.

Brianne punched the button and whispered, "Come on, come on. Second floor…main floor, oh man, be empty…"

The doors opened, and she blew out a breath. Her adrenaline thrust the gurney against the back wall, and the elevator swayed.

"What are you doing?" Boone sounded drunk.

"Sorry, I'm...nervous." She hit the close button, then main floor. "We'll be fine."

"Okay, fine."

"Please, no one be there," Brianne chanted as she stood behind the gurney, ready to burst out of the utility elevator and race to the main elevator, of which she didn't have a clue where that was.

The doors opened and she shoved with all her might. Boone wiggled as it went over the elevator door tracks and sent several robot parts over the side.

"I want off this thing," Boone garbled.

"No, no." Brianne patted him. "Just a little longer."

"You're a wild driver."

"Sorry." She spotted exits signs and hoped that meant an elevator. They went down a dimly lit corridor, and Brianne blazed past an elevator sign in an intersection. She stiffened her legs and tried to navigate the corner but slid by.

Boone almost rolled off the top, and more limbs clattered to the floor. "Sorry."

"Don't say that if you don't mean it."

"We're almost there!"

"I certainly hope so."

Brianne heard the utility elevator ring and prayed they didn't have unwanted company. With all the body parts falling from the gurney, they were leaving a well-marked trail. At the next intersection, the elevator sign pointed left. Brianne went wide and took the corner faster than she should have. The gurney's right side slammed into the wall.

"Oh, for crying out loud!" Boone tried to get up. "Let me drive."

Brianne shoved him down. "Don't move!"

There was the elevator, next to lockers that she now remembered seeing when she arrived. Several footsteps were picking up the pace behind them. The gurney was moving so fast that Brianne wasn't able to slow it down before it crashed into the wall next to the elevator.

Brianne slammed the button. She looked to the right, and a cluster of guards was coming through the hall seventy feet away. To the left, another group was rounding the corner to the adjacent hall, fifty feet away.

Boone had fallen off the gurney and was sitting in front of the elevator door trying to untangle the bed sheet from his body. It took an eternity for the elevator to come from the lower floors.

All three groups of humbots were converging on them, and the doors finally opened with the barber chair sitting in the middle of it.

"Oh, thank God!"

Brianne hopped over Boone and lifted under his armpits. Boone pushed with his legs sending Brianne flying into the barber chair with Boone on top. Just as the door was five inches from closing, a robot part wedged between them forcing the door open.

Boone kicked the hand out and punched the close button. A conglomeration of stampeding robots collided in front of the elevator. Many of them tried to untangle enough to place any part of their body between the doors. Finally the doors completely closed.

Boone and Brianne stared vacantly at the elevator doors as the barber chair descended.

CHAPTER 22
Reconciling

———

Logan moved from the waiting room chair when the barber chair started rising on its own. Brianne had been gone fifteen minutes and Boone thirty-five. A mist fell as the chair penetrated the bubble it formed in the ceiling. The chair disappeared, and then nothing happened.

A car slowly drove by so Logan closed the drape then returned in front of the barber chair glued to his spot, praying that both Boone and Brianne would come back safely.

Why is it taking so long to come back?

Finally a mist gently fell as the ceiling bubbled out into the room. Logan smiled when he saw two sets of feet. *Why is Boone sitting on top of Brianne?*

When they finally broke free of the bubble, Boone hopped off the chair and waited for the chair to settle to the floor. He grabbed the haircloth that was covered in freshly cut hair and tore it off of his neck.

"We've got to go back and free the rest of the kids," Boone spoke with urgency.

Brianne scanned Boone up and down. "Boone, you're all human."

"All human?" Logan questioned.

Boone looked in the mirror and touched his chest and legs. "And I'm not drugged!"

"Drugged?" Logan repeated.

"And my hair is cut! How'd you do that, Mr. Payne?"

"I didn't." Logan eyed Boone's cut. "It's the best cut I've ever seen on you."

Boone didn't even hear what he said. "We've got to go back and help, Bree."

"I want to check on Dexter."

"How long have we been gone?"

"You've been gone thirty-five minutes and Brianne fifteen."

"You're kidding," Boone and Brianne said in unison.

"No."

"You're right, Bree. I need to talk to Dexter, then we're getting help to rescue those other kids."

"We need a ride to the hospital." Brianne looked at Logan.

"My next two appointments canceled. I'm all yours because I need to find out where you two went and what you learned."

Logan quickly closed the barbershop and led them to his silver GMC pickup.

By the time they pulled into Mountain View Hospital parking lot, Boone filled in Logan to the point where Brianne arrived.

"I'll drop you off and return after three. I want the rest of the story."

Brianne and Boone hustled into the hospital and were soon in Dexter's room. Boone moved to a chair next to Dexter. His hand shook as he placed it on Dexter's arm that housed his IV. Brianne sat in the chair at the foot of the bed.

"Hey, Dex," Boone spoke softly. "I bet you never thought I'd be visiting you." His laugh was laced with nerves. "I can't tell you how sorry I am for how I treated you. I had no right to terrorize you by holding you over the canal by the strands of your hair."

Brianne gasped. When he saw tears flooding her eyes, he fought to control his emotions.

"I heard your cries as I walked away from you and I..." Boone bit his lower lip and paused. When he continued, his voice was raspy. "I did nothing. After I rescue some other kids I just met...it's another story...I'm going to turn myself in, and you'll never have to be afraid of me again. I'll be your best protector."

A knot caught in Boone's throat when he saw tears streaming down Brianne's face. She shook her head with compassion on her face. Boone bowed his head next to Dexter's arm and swallowed a sob.

"Just be…my…friend," a whisper came from Dexter.

Brianne raced to the other side of Dexter's bed. "Hey, buddy." Brianne smiled as she grabbed his hand. "Welcome back."

"I'm really thirsty."

Brianne lifted the pitcher and found it empty. "Let me tell them you're awake." Brianne squeezed Dexter's hand and left.

Dexter looked apprehensively at Boone.

"So do you mean it, Dex?"

"Yes." Dexter's voice was hoarse. "Friendship is all I want from anyone."

"I can't tell you how sorry I am. There's no excuse for what I did."

"We all make mistakes, Boone. I just wish your whopper of a mistake hadn't included me."

"No kidding. You can bet it won't happen again."

Two nurses, the doctor, and Brianne entered the room, so Boone moved to a corner and just observed.

After they poked and prodded Dexter to make sure he would keep conscious, they insisted that Boone and Brianne let him rest.

They went to the waiting room in silence and waited for Logan to return.

"You seem totally different, Boone. After listening to what you told Mr. Payne, I can understand why, but I don't understand why you started."

"It seems stupid now."

"I want to understand."

"My dad is always so busy with work it seems like he doesn't care about me. He's missed some things in my life that I really wanted him to be there. I was angry. I turned that anger outwardly to anyone weaker than I was."

"I'm sorry you feel neglected, Boone."

"The funny thing is, every one of the guys I met at the Robotic Center said their dads were absent from their lives for many different reasons. We all were angry and turned that anger outward instead of dealing with the issue.

"I'm so sorry for harassing you and stalking you. That was totally wrong. When you did your whole makeover thing, you knocked me off of my feet. I just went way overboard trying to draw your attention."

Brianne didn't say anything.

"Please forgive me for hurting someone you deeply care about because I was jealous, Bree." Boone placed her hand in his. "I promise I will never intentionally hurt you again."

Brianne wiped her face and squeezed Boone's hand. "I forgive you. The hardest part will be forgiving yourself."

Logan entered the hospital and hesitated when he saw Brianne crying.

"Is Dexter all right?"

"Yes!" Brianne hugged him. "He's out of the coma. He's just resting now.

"Okay, I'll come back and visit him another time. Are we ready to go home? I'm eager to hear what happened after you got to the Robotics Center, Brianne."

"Yeah, let's go," Boone said.

Brianne finished her part as they followed Logan into the barbershop.

At Boone's insistence, they decided to help the other children who were still trapped at the Robotics Center. If it had not been for Logan's curiosity, he wouldn't have let them talk him into it.

Boone sat in the barber chair with Brianne on his lap.

"Are you ready for this?" Logan asked before he pressed the hydraulic lift.

"More than I was the first time," Boone answered.

"I'm not sure I am, but here goes." Logan pressed the hydraulic lift and the chair rose until it reached its normal extension, and stopped.

"So those kids are stuck there forever?" Boone asked.

"I don't know how God works in most things, but could it be that you two just had an experience orchestrated by God to help you get over these milestones in your life?"

"What do you mean, Mr. P.?"

"Well, the Angel that spoke to me said that the children who had struggles in their life and needed some help would ask me, 'How high does this chair go?' Our God is an amazing God. Is it possible that those children weren't real but only agents used to help you discover things about yourself?"

"Hey, Boone. Did you see the humbots' faces just before they collided in front of the door?"

"Yeah. I saw Sawyer, Taylor, Dallas, Joe and…"

"Don't you remember? What happened to their faces just before they all fell to the floor?"

Boone paused for a moment. "Their faces disappeared!"

"Disappeared?" Logan said. "What do you mean?"

"As I made eye contact with them." Brianne got out of the barber chair. "It was like their facial features melted into a smooth surface."

Logan nodded. "Yep, I'd say this was all for your benefits."

"It seemed just as real as things are now," Brianne said.

"As you grow closer to God, you'll discover that this life isn't as real as the spiritual life that surrounds Him."

"No one's ever going to believe this." Boone stood.

"Could you do me a favor?" Logan asked.

"What?"

"Let's keep this between ourselves. I don't know how often a child will come here when they need help. Now that I understand it more, I won't be so mystified and terrified."

Brianne lifted her right hand up, palm down. "Our secret?"

Boone put his right hand over Brianne's, then Logan moved in to cover both of their hands. "Our secret," Logan and Boone said.

"So how'd my hair get cut?"

"I don't have all the answers. If anything I'm an instigator of more questions."

They all laughed, and then grew quiet.

"Well, I have something to do." Boone made his way to the door. "I'm going to mow the lawn, and then tell my mom what I've done. Then I'm going to call Officer Nutt to turn myself in."

"Do you want me to come?" Brianne asked.

"I appreciate your willingness, but I want to do this alone."

When he opened the door, Brianne rushed to his side and hugged him. "I'm your friend, Boone, don't forget that."

"Thanks." Boone left with tears glistening.

Logan and Brianne watched Boone until he walked out of view.

"What do you think will happen to him?"

"It's hard to tell. I'm sure community service will be part of his sentence, but it depends on what Dexter and his parents decide. Whatever he faces, from what he just experienced, I'm positive he'll handle it just fine."

"Yep. I'm sure you're right."

Leave A Review

Thanks for downloading this book. If you enjoyed reading it, please leave a review. Your input helps others decide to read this book and helps the author on future books.

Author's Biography

Kathy Rae lives in Spokane Valley, Washington, and ran her own barber business for thirty-five years. Working with people provided an endless avenue of inspiration for new books. Besides reading and writing, Kathy loves carpentry, landscaping, music, and anything that involves creating. If she is creating, she is a happy woman!

Kathy has taken a course in Institute for Children's Literature, is active in several author organizations in the Spokane area, and is a member of Jerry Jenkins Writer's Guild.

Kathy's first book, *The Jewel of Hope: Book 1 of The Hope Trilogy,* was published in 2014. K.Rae Kreations published Kathy's second book, *Ducky Day or Yucky Day ~ You Choose,* in 2015. K.Rae Kreations also published in 2016 an Adult Coloring Book series including,

Stained Glass Windows and U.S. Military Monuments and in 2017, *Snatching Hope Away: Book 2 of The Hope Trilogy.*

If you enjoyed *Deprogramming A Bully*, please leave a review on the site you purchase it. Your input is valuable to other readers and Kathy!

Visit YouTube under *Kathy Rae* for book trailers and songs that I sing.

Kathy's website is **http://www.kathyrae.net/wordpress1**.

https://www.facebook.com/kathy.rae.5 directs you to Kathy Rae's Facebook page.

Kathy Rae can be found on LinkedIn and Twitter, as well.

Coming Soon

OTHER BOOKS COMING SOON!

THE CHILDREN COLORING STORYBOOK SERIES:
FLIPPIN' AND A FLOPPIN' FLAPS

HELP! MY MESSY ROOM SWALLOWED MY SISTER

DON'T BE SASSIN' THE MOOSE

THE BARBER CHAIR SERIES –
BOOK 2:
THE ART OF ESCAPE

BOOK 3:
THE ULTIMATE CALLING VIDEO GAME

THE HOPE TRILOGY –
BOOK 3:
HOPE RESTORED

What Inspired The Series

It was 1985, in Spokane, Washington at *The Cut of Gold* barbershop when a father dropped his son off for a haircut. As he rushed to the chair with excitement he asked, "how high does this chair go?"

After telling me what he wanted for the cut, I was hard pressed to concentrate on anything he said because a book was brewing in my heart.

Fast-forward to 2015, and another boy walked into *Taylor'd Cuts Barbershop* in Shelley, Idaho, also owned and operated by me. He also asked, "How high does this chair go?"

That re-ignited the flame that had begun in 1985. I had the beginning of this book the next day.

With bullying being such a prevalent problem today, I chose to kick off the series with that difficulty and gave a bit of a twist by writing it in the bully's viewpoint.

This series is especially fun because I place so many things I love about Shelley, Idaho in the book and the characters are the names of people I have met while cutting hair.

The barber in this series is a person in my life who will not be revealed at this time. Needless to say, I am having a lot of fun writing this series! I pray that you have enjoyed it. There are many more to come, so hold on tight.

God bless you all,

Kathy Rae